Andrew, the Big Deal

Andrew the Big Deal

Barbara Brooks Wallace

Jacket Painting by Joann Daley

Follett Publishing Company
Chicago

Library of Congress Catalog Card Number: 76-93809

ISBN 0-695-40111-4 Titan binding
ISBN 0-695-80111-2 Trade binding

Weekly Reader Children's Book Club Edition
Senior Division

For my son Jimmy, with love and ten percent.

One

I'VE HEARD that when things get really bad, they can't go anyplace but up. I have news for the person who invented that saying. He hadn't met me. I could start with the day I was born to explain what I mean, but that would be too depressing. So I'll just start with last August when we left California to come to Washington, D.C.

In the first place, no one wanted to leave California —not Dad, not Mom, not Micky, not Beege, not Migsy, and not yours truly. Especially not yours truly, Andrew. This was mostly because of a new guy who moved into our block in Van Nuys. I'd never had a guy to goof around with in my whole life. Most guys get one about every time they turn around. Even little teeny guys are always running around with someone having adventures and all that. I've read this a lot. I don't make friends very easily. You might say I hardly make friends at all. Anyway, this guy's name is Jay. I told him I'd write him a letter, and I did. But I figured he'd never answer it.

Micky, that's Michael Eldridge Kellogg, my eighteen-year-old brother, turned out to be the lucky one. He stayed in California. That's because he finally got himself accepted at U.C.L.A. I guess he was lucky to get in with *his* grades. He was having to be tutored all over the place his last year in high school. Anyway, he ended up getting a scholarship, mostly for football. Rah!

I don't mean to sound stingy about this piece of information. It's just that I personally don't have enough muscle or coordination to shoot a crummy marble. I even get clobbered at tiddlywinks by Migsy. That's Mary Katherine Kellogg, my kid sister who's just turned seven. This is pretty embarrassing for a twelve-year-old guy. That's yours truly, Andrew Schofield Kellogg.

Anyway, about California. Usually, nobody in our family minds leaving a place. My dad is in the Air Force. Every three or four years he gets orders, and we have to move. So we move. I don't mean that every time we go we're all jumping around with joy. It's just that it's no big deal. This time, everyone practically went into shock, even Mom. She started going to pieces over the news as soon as Dad announced it back in June. It wasn't leaving California that bugged her so much, though, as the idea of going to Washington, D.C. We'd heard that everything was bad there—housing, shopping, schools, etc., etc. And you had to be millionaires to live there, which we weren't. But for the rest of us, it was mostly leaving California that mattered.

Beege, that's William Barnes Kellogg, Jr., my sixteen-year-old brother—and don't ask me how come *he* got to be the junior and not Micky—was pretty friendly with a girl who lived next door to us named Stella. Her mom and dad were putting a swimming pool in their backyard, and the whole Kellogg family was invited to use it any time they wanted to. Everyone in our family is this big swimmer, even Migsy. She cuts through the water like a little tadpole. I swim like a loose wet noodle, but I like it. It's the only sport I like. So you can see that leaving all this cool, clear, blue, luscious water that was going to lie practically at our back door was a pretty cruel blow.

Then on top of it all, Mom got sick. One of the kids in a family in our neighborhood busted his head and had to go to the hospital. The mother, who was a widow, wanted to go visit him but couldn't find anyone to stay with the rest of her kids. My mom is the kind who is always running around doing good works. Dad calls her the Mother Superior of the neighborhood. In five minutes, Mom was over there taking care of the kids, who all had colds, it turned out. Mom got their cold, and before anyone knew it, it had turned into pneumonia. This was the week before we were supposed to go to Washington. It was three weeks before we finally left, and even then Mom wasn't feeling too hot. I guess it didn't help much, being sick when she was already worried about the big move we were going to make.

We had already sold our house, but it almost came unsold when the people who bought it got nasty and said that if we didn't move out according to schedule, they might consider refusing to buy the house. Dad told them in this icy voice that people don't get well on schedule. He said he was sorry we were inconveniencing them, but if that was the way they felt, perhaps they had better cancel the contract. They backed down finally and said they would wait. The good old Samaritans! I mean, they were already in an apartment and could easily wait a few more days.

But all this made Mom feel even worse. Once I walked into her room and caught her wiping tears away from her face. I hate to see Mom cry, but I didn't blame her.

"Maybe we won't have to go," Migsy said one day. We were sitting on the fence watching the workmen in Stella's backyard getting ready to build the swimming pool. The fence practically had holes along the top where we'd been sitting and leaning ever since the men had started work.

"We'll go, all right," I said.

"Next week like we planned?" Migsy asked.

"Look, stupid, you know Mom isn't going to be well enough to travel next week."

Migsy is this big thinker. She really is. I watched her stare off into Stella's yard. After a while, I finally found out what she was thinking about.

"Is the Air Force going to fire Daddy?" she asked me.

"Fire Dad? What in heck for?" I answered.

"Because we're going to be late getting to Washington."

"Migsy, the Air Force doesn't go around firing people

when someone gets sick and can't help anything, for Pete's sake. What kind of outfit do you think Dad works for? Anyway, we'll only be a couple of weeks late."

After this, Migsy went off into space again. She put her hands under her chin and stared harder at the beginning of the hole in the ground that was going to be Stella's gorgeous swimming pool.

"Does this mean we're not going to have our holiday?"

"I guess not. Staying around here waiting for Mom to get well is using up the extra weeks Dad was going to take for leave. We'll just have to go right from here to there."

Then Migsy stayed quiet for so long that I had to say something more. "Look, it isn't the worst thing in the world not getting to see the Grand Canyon or go to New York or any of those places. We'll probably get to go another time. Besides," I went on, feeling brilliant because I'd thought of it, "if we wait here long enough, we may get to use Stella's pool before we leave."

Migsy shrugged. I admitted to myself that her shrug had a point. At the rate they were building that pool, we'd have to wear crash helmets if we went into it before we left because we'd be diving into solid concrete. I thought I'd better add something else.

"One more thing, Butch. If you say anything to Mom, or cry, or anything stupid like that, I'll clobber you!"

Migsy gave me this blank look of hers. Then she raised her eyebrows and screwed her lips together. I figured by this that she got the message. We stared some more into what was going to be Stella's swimming pool. Suddenly Migsy jumped off the fence into our yard and ran toward the front of the house. I wasn't surprised at this, because I'd heard Micky's VW pull into the driveway. Micky is this big hero of Migsy's. I don't blame her much, big football star and all that. Beege is her next hero in line. He's a baseball star. Basketball in winter. That should make me hero number three, which is a joke, in case you didn't notice it. When we went up to Big Bear, I couldn't even stay on a sled. Not to mention the situation of getting beat at tiddlywinks. Some athlete!

All I am is good in school. I don't mean that I'm a genius or anything. It's just that I've been bringing home A's and marks like that ever since first grade. Except for handwriting. That's just the trouble. No surprises. I never get presents for improvement, because what kind of big deal is it if you improve your rotten penmanship. Not that I could. I'm even uncoordinated pushing a pencil. Anyway, my family is numb to the whole business of my good grades, like I was this shot of novocaine or something. I bet they'd put up a statue of me if I ever hit a lousy baseball, though.

Oh well, I guess they're right. Who ever heard of a straight-A hero? Especially a guy. I couldn't blame Migsy.

Anyway, it was her hero Micky, in the end, who made leaving California about as tough as anything could be. Not that he did anything rotten. It was just that Micky was Mom's first kid, and here we were going off and leaving him behind. He wasn't exactly suffering, going off to U.C.L.A. to play football and maybe do a little studying while he was living at his best buddy's house. It was Mom who suffered. I've personally never had any kids, so I wouldn't know about it, but I read once that if you're the first kid in a family, you're always the big deal. Besides, Micky was the first kid in our family to leave home.

Mom tried to be brave about it, but you could see that she was putting it on. I didn't believe the act one minute. The last time Micky drove off in his VW, just before we left, Mom's eyes weren't red as plums for nothing.

I thought that maybe staying over I'd get to see more of Jay before we moved, but he and his family went down to Laguna for two weeks, so that was that. I just moped around with Migsy most of the time. Grover, who is our multi-type brown and black and white dog, drooped all over the place with agony. Dogs kill me the way they know when something weird is going on. As for Beege, he was away most of the time playing in a baseball tournament with his team. He wasn't even around to help pack the car the last day because he had some big game going on. Baseball games and things like that are good excuses for getting out of just about everything in our family.

You should have seen our station wagon the day we left. The moving company had already taken all our furniture and the big stuff, but there was still a lot of junk left over. The back seat was piled to the roof with kids and bags and dog, and even the roof of the car was covered with a big mountain of stuff strapped on. The back bumper was practically dragging on the ground from the weight. We looked pretty junky. Beege got red when Stella came out to tell him good-bye.

We were all joking about the way our car looked. No one really felt much like joking, though. This was because we knew that Mom, even though she tried to pretend that she felt fine, really felt pretty rotten. As soon as she got in the car, Dad propped a bed pillow under her head up in front, and she just kind of sat there, pale and gone-looking, with her arm around Grover, who'd jumped up beside her. Mom is not the pale, gone type. Watching her scared me.

As we chugged away from the house, I looked over toward her from my seat behind Dad and saw Grover licking her face. He was licking tears off her cheek. She gave him a big, tight squeeze. I knew this was really a squeeze for Micky.

Then I did something I'd promised myself I wouldn't do. I turned my head and gave our old house one more quick look. What happened was that I caught sight of something I didn't care to see. That was the big hole in the ground filled with wet concrete that was going to be Stella's rotten old swimming pool.

Two

THE TRIP east wasn't too bad, considering. I like traveling, especially having breakfast in coffee shops. When we're traveling, Dad and Mom let us order anything we want to eat, practically. I always order an omelette and English muffins. Also, they don't scream when I order tea. Beege had to tease me about my little tea and crumpets every time, though. I wished he'd go drown.

One interesting thing happened. I mean, besides the flat tire on the freeway. That was the day Grover got loose when we were leading him from the motel kennel to the car. He started after some cat who was hanging around the swimming pool, and was going so fast he skidded on the cement. Zoom! Right into the pool! We got him out right away, but the motel manager didn't think it was as interesting an event as we did. He was muttering something about maybe having to drain the pool. What's wrong with a guy like that? Grover's a perfectly clean, decent dog. A couple of times he's jumped into the bathtub with me, and I didn't go and drain the tub right away, for Pete's sake. Not until I'd finished washing, anyway. And I didn't even make him get out until I did. That motel guy must be some kind of person.

The weather wasn't bad most of the way, but it was pouring down rain the day we pulled into Washington, hot and muggy. When the rain got around to stopping once or twice, the city looked as if it was being boiled in gray steam. That figured. Everyone had told us the climate around Washington was crummy along with everything else.

Of course, people also told us what a great experience it would be for us kids living near all these historical buildings and monuments. Now, I don't mean to sound disrespectful and against the government or anything like that, but how many kids would rather live near a bunch of crummy historical buildings than have this luscious swimming pool practically in their backyard?

Anyway, I was sitting in the back seat between Migsy and Beege because it was my turn not to get the window, and thinking about all this for the one millionth time. I was just peering around Migsy's head trying to catch one of these famous views when a truck roared by, sending a big wave of muddy water over the side of the car. It was like the truck was giving me a big, mud raspberry for my trouble. Welcome to Washington, buddy!

I didn't give up but kept looking while the dirty brown sheet of water finished sliding down the window. Everyone in the car was quiet. It was a gloomy quiet, if you know what I mean. Migsy put her head down on my shoulder and started rubbing her cheek against my T-shirt. "I'm tired. I hate this place." Migs had been pretty good through the whole trip, so I decided not to clobber her. Anyway, Mom had her head against the bed pillow, and her eyes were closed. I didn't think she'd heard Migsy.

Suddenly I got this big idea. "Hey, look," I said, kind of quietly so I wouldn't wake Mom. "Look! There's the Lincoln Memorial! Wow!"

"Where? Where?" Migsy asked. She was pretty excited.

"Yeah, where, Andrew?" Beege asked, forgetting to sound bored for a change.

"Right out there." I pointed out the window to the first thing I could see up ahead.

"That's just an old gas station," Migsy said.

"Well, how about that? Foiled again!" I said.

Migsy busted out crying.

Beege shoved me in the ribs. Hard. "Oh, shut up, Andrew. You're a real comedian."

Nothing is exactly hysterical when you're hot and tired and slightly miserable. I guess I wasn't very funny. I have to admit it. But Beege didn't have to poke me so hard. The big crumb! He never missed an opportunity.

Dad wasn't mad at me, though. "Hey, don't jump too hard on Andrew," he said. "He just reminded me we need gas. Right now, as a matter of fact, or we may end up stranded somewhere on a bridge over the Potomac. I missed the Lincoln Memorial back there so I guess I'll just pull in here to the Smithsonian Institution."

"Hey, where, Dad?" I hollered. If there was one thing I *did* want to see in Washington, it was the Smithsonian. Naturally, Dad was just giving me the business, and we were only turning into another gas station. I had it coming. Anyway, it turned off Migsy's tears, and she started to giggle. Migsy is this great giggler.

Funny, Mom hadn't wakened up through all the noise, but the feel of the car stopping must have done it. She raised her head and looked around, kind of startled.

"Where are we? Are we there?"

"Not yet, Sam. Just stopping for gas." Sam is what Dad calls Mom. Her real name is Sarah.

"Oh," Mom said, dropping her head back down on the pillow. Then she raised up again suddenly and turned to look at us. "Everyone okay back there?"

"Sure," we all said. I poked Migsy just in case.

Mom put her head back down and just kind of stared out the window. She'd been pale and limp like that almost all the way across the country. Mom's not like that. She's usually pretty excited about coming to a new place. I figured she'd even be excited about Washington once we got there.

No one needed to get out of the car at the gas station to get a drink of water or anything like that. This is rare in our family, because someone almost always has to get out for something, if you know what I mean. Of course, the pouring down rain probably had something to do with this. I personally would rather stay in the car and suffer than get out and get drowned. So we just got our gas and pulled out.

"How much farther do we have to go, Dad?" Beege asked.

"You've got me," Dad said. "This is the first time I've ever driven through the District."

"But you've been to Washington before, haven't you, Daddy?" Migsy asked.

"Oh sure, Piglet, lots of times. On temporary duty."

I should mention that Dad often calls Migsy names out of *Winnie the Pooh*, which is Migsy's favorite bunch of stories, even though she already has a pretty good nickname. Everyone in our family has a nickname except me. I've always been just Andrew. Once in a while someone calls me "the professor." It's better than nothing.

But that isn't all of it. They also call me "the absentminded professor." Maybe it's the absentminded part of it that makes them treat me the way they do. The thing is, though, that I'm not really absentminded. It's just that they can't think of anything else that fits what I do. What I do is dream up this crazy stuff. Like when I was a teeny guy and dug this little hole in the backyard to trap Santa Claus because I was mad at him, only Dad stepped into it and sprained his ankle. It's probably a good thing I had it all figured out that old S. C. was a midget elf, or I would have dug a hole big enough for Dad to fall in and sprain his neck.

Then there was the time I placed a bunch of calls to the police department about some burglars that were breaking into an empty house near us in Van Nuys. The only problem was that the burglars turned out to be this old lady who was feeding these people's cat while they were away. The police came out anyway and had a few words with Mom and Dad about me.

But it wasn't until I sneaked out of the house every night for about ten nights to spot these weird Martians and then nearly got pneumonia that I swore I'd never imagine a bunch of boloney again. The problem is, I never think I'm imagining it. I just always find these significant-type clues. Then I start having conversations with myself. I can't explain how it happens after that, but I can end up convincing myself of just about anything.

One of my teachers said I had a splendid imagination. Mom and Dad said they hoped I recovered from it, which sounded like I had some crummy disease. I don't blame them, though. One of the big things I told myself when we left California was, "Never again!" I mean, no more clues, no more conversations with myself, no more imagination when we got to Washington. There was going to be a new Andrew Kellogg, and I wasn't kidding.

"Can't you even guess how much longer it's going to be, Dad?" Beege asked again.

"Sorry, Beege. All I *do* know is that if I hadn't missed that turnoff to the Beltway, we wouldn't have to be fighting all this traffic and probably doubling our time getting there."

Everyone in the back seat groaned. Migsy sighed. "I guess I'm thirsty."

"Guess again," I said.

"Okay, I'm hungry."

"Very good. Have a pretzel."

Mom suddenly came to life in the front seat. "Do we still have those? I'll take one after you blow out the moths." She reached a hand over the back of the seat and signaled me. When Mom makes a joke, even if it's a small one, you know she's feeling okay. Then you're not so scared anymore.

"I have a few," I said. I reached down to the floor and started rummaging around behind my feet where I'd hidden the package.

Beege had to put in his two cents. "He still has *his* package. He's been hoarding it since yesterday, naturally."

"Go choke," I mentioned under my breath. I am this great hoarder, though. I have to admit it. But Beege's attitude was strictly live today and live off everyone else tomorrow. He made me sick. "Well, just because I'm smart enough to pick one of Howard Johnson's bottomless bags," I said, coming up with my beat-up cellophane package of pretzels. First I handed one each to Mom and Dad, and then I generously passed the bag around the back seat. I mean, even to Beege. I wondered if I should get my head examined.

Grover, who was up in front with Mom, heard the cellophane crunching around and leaped back on top of me. Grover would give his tail for a pretzel. I gave him a couple for nothing, though.

After that, everything turned gloomy again as Dad plowed through the traffic, and we tried to see something through the rain. Beege pulled his guitar case out from under his feet and spread it all over me while he opened it. Then he started to plunk some kind of crummy tune on his precious guitar, waving the neck all around in front of my face and practically poking my eye out.

It wasn't the guitar, though, that kept me from looking out the window. I have to be honest. I had my nose halfway in a book, and was also goofing around with Grover. So it was Migsy who saw it first after I'd practically ruined my eyeballs staring out the window all that time to see something famous. It was the Washington Monument. We'd told Migsy all about it, and she'd seen pictures of it. She nearly had a fit. Dad slowed down so we could get a better look.

As we were pulling slowly past the Monument, Dad said, "Andrew, if you can take the time to look to the left, I think you'll see something that just might be of interest to you." It was the Smithsonian! I couldn't believe that it was there, right in front of my nose. We were looking at the Museum of History and Technology, which is only a part of it. Boy, it takes months to go through that place.

I didn't think I'd see anything more exciting than that, but I did, the dome of the Capitol building. Everyone in the car was so quiet you wouldn't believe it. It really makes you feel solemn the first time you see it.

After that we saw the Jefferson Memorial and the Pentagon. The Pentagon is where Dad works. I'd seen pictures of it at least a million times, but I'd never thought of it as being a real place.

All the rest of the way to our motel in Alexandria, I was feeling pretty patriotic. And I kept thinking how this was my country, and how I would run away from home and lie about my age and do these big, brave, heroic acts. I didn't know what kind of acts exactly, but there are probably a bunch around that you can do. I mean, let's face it, what chance has a twelve-year-old guy got to be a hero at home? Especially a guy like me.

I was thinking about all these noble deeds so hard that I forgot about not wanting to come to Washington. In fact, I practically managed to forget about Stella's lousy old swimming pool.

The good feeling I had didn't last very long. It disappeared the next morning, and I forgot all about this big patriot I was going to be. The next morning was when we went to look for a house.

Dad called up this real estate office right after he got back from signing in at the Pentagon, and we all piled into the real estate guy's car to go house hunting. Except for Grover. We'd taken him to the vet's practically the minute after we arrived at the motel. Someday I'm going to own a swanky motel that just takes dogs. I mean it. Then their people can go stay in these crummy cages someplace.

At the real estate office we found out that because we'd been late getting to Washington and it was practically time for school to start, just about all the good houses had been bought. And there wasn't anything at all left to rent that our family could squeeze into. What was left for us to look at, especially in Alexandria where Mom and Dad wanted to live, was pretty sickening. This made Mom feel even worse, because it was her pneumonia that had made us so late in getting there.

The creepy character who took us around to see the houses didn't help much either. His name was Plunkard.

You could have had a better conversation with a Chesapeake Bay clam. I mean, even though you don't want someone going around trying to sell you your own back teeth, you sort of like him to say something, for Pete's sake. He didn't even have any expression on his face. About as much as a poker chip. I don't mean that he wasn't honest or anything like that. It's just that he knew Mom and Dad were dying to get out of our expensive motel and into a house as soon as possible. Also, that Mom and Dad had been told by a bunch of people that the place where he was showing them houses had about the best schools around for all three of us kids. You can practically sell my parents a tree house if it's near a good school. Mr. Plunkard knew it. You should have seen the stuff he showed us.

He called the house that Mom and Dad finally bought a colonial style. It sure was colonial! They must have brought it over on the *Mayflower*, piece by piece. I have to be honest, though. It wasn't Mr. Plunkard's fault that it finally boiled down to being the only house that was big enough and cheap enough for us.

"Well, at least it has enough bedrooms," Mom said kind of weakly as we fumbled our way down the dark stairs. Her tone of voice told us that this was probably the house we were going to have to live in.

"But it's so dark!" Migsy groaned. All the houses we'd looked at were dark next to our California house, but this was the darkest. They could have used it for a model on a horror show.

"That can always be corrected with a few cans of white paint," Dad said, trying to sound as if he meant it.

"I think we'd better have a look at the basement," he said next to Mr. Plunkard. I don't know how Mr. Plunkard kept his face screwed on at this.

There were a couple of places in the basement where Dad couldn't even stand up straight. He tried it and cracked his head on a water pipe. Also, something else looked suspicious.

"Could that be a water line around the wall?" he asked Mr. Plunkard. Well, if you'd asked me, it didn't exactly look as if someone had painted on those lines for decoration.

Mr. Plunkard just shrugged and rolled his eyeballs off into space. That's what I mean about him. A real conversationalist. Anyway, whether the basement had ever been flooded or not practically didn't make any difference anymore. Old poker-chip face didn't have to say anything. If Mom and Dad wanted a house, this had to be it.

After we left the basement, Mom and Dad started talking to Mr. Plunkard about boring stuff like down payments and mortgages and taxes. Migsy and I decided we'd cut out of there and see if we could discover any more miserable features of our new house. I wanted to look over the room I figured was going to be my bedroom. My crystal ball told me this because it was the room that was farthest away from the bathroom, of which this glorious house has only one. I had a picture of myself never getting a turn in it and ending up the scummiest kid in the neighborhood.

But before we left the others, Migsy said this dumb thing. "Do you think we can ever have a pool in our yard?"

We all knew she meant a swimming pool, and it was too stupid to answer. I didn't even feel like taking the time to clobber her.

But Mr. Plunkard finally got conversational. "Oh, didn't you notice the little pool in the backyard?" he said.

Migsy never stopped to ask him any questions. "Oh boy!" she shouted, and ran out. I felt a little excited myself, even though I didn't see how we could have missed anything like a pool, for Pete's sake, when we were in the backyard. I ran out after her while Beege sauntered along behind us. He wouldn't lower himself to get excited about anything *I* thought was neat.

There was a pool there, all right, just around the bend of the house where no one had gone. A pool for fish. It was nothing more than a lousy old fishpond.

It wasn't even a decent fishpond, either. It looked more like a garbage dump. There were a bunch of rusty tin cans lying around on the bottom, and slimy green stuff was growing on everything. Also, this dead goldfish was floating around on top of the water with his big blown-up stomach sticking out like a rotten, old balloon. It made me kind of sick to watch him.

Migsy looked as if she was going to bust out crying. I guess she would have, except that suddenly we heard a loud kerchunk, kerchunk from the middle of the pool. Sitting there on this moldy pile of rocks was a huge old bullfrog. Kerchunk, kerchunk, he went again. I think he was trying to talk to us.

"Kerchunk, kerchunk, to you too, boy," Beege said.

"Hey, that's a glorious-looking frog," I added.

"Glorious," Migsy shouted. "That's what I'm going to call him. Glorious! He's going to be my new pet."

"Oh, I don't know about that," I said, looking this Glorious over carefully. "I might just use him for a scientific experiment. You know, kind of—pickle him. How would you like that, Glorious, old buddy, ending up a little old dill pickle?" Glorious kerchunked and gave me a nasty look.

"You're not going to pickle him! He's going to be my pet!" Migsy said, stamping her foot at me. She was grinning, though, because she knows I have a brain like a marshmallow when it comes to animals. The only stuff I could ever cut up in biology is junk that's already dead when you buy it.

"Hey, Migs," I said, "we can clean up this old pool and make a nice home for Glor. Would you like that?"

Migsy began to clap her hands and jump around like crazy.

Beege smiled in his usual superior way. "A good idea, Andrew, old man. I'll even offer a little supervision and some professional advice along the way."

You could bet that was all Beege would offer, but it was better than nothing from *him*.

Anyway, it was nice to have something to be excited about for a change, and Migsy and I started making big plans for Glorious. We were having such a good time over it that I didn't pay much attention to Mom's complaining that it was all her fault that we had to end up buying this "dump," as she called it. And it wasn't until that night when I walked into Mom and Dad's motel room and found out Mom had been crying again, that I knew how bad she really felt about it.

Three

WE COULDN'T move into the house until Monday, so we had Sunday with nothing much to do. That was okay with us kids, because we wanted to do some sight-seeing. It was okay with Mom and Dad, too, except they said we had better go to church first. With Mom sick in California, we'd been kind of sloppy about getting to church. Mom said we were going to start out on the right foot in our new home. I'm personally mixed-up about church. What I mean is, most Sundays I'd rather stay home and sleep. I have to be honest. Mom is right, though. When you go to church, you usually feel better. I don't know why. Once in a while, your mom and dad know something.

We decided we'd go to Christ Church in Alexandria.

That's where George Washington went. We sat in a pew that had this little brass plate on it that said it was where General Robert E. Lee sat. When he was living, I mean. It made me feel weird when I stopped to think about it, kind of historical and dead, if you know what I mean.

We liked Christ Church. The minister was pretty nice, and Migsy liked the crazy little swinging doors into the pews. Dad had trouble with his long legs, though. He said that George Washington must have been a pygmy to fit into the pews, or maybe had pretzels for legs so he could bend them all up when he was kneeling to pray. This really killed me, thinking about old G. W. walking around on a couple of pretzels.

We decided to make it a George Washington day, and after church, we went to the Monument in Washington. Beege, Migsy, and I walked up the stairs, but Mom and Dad took the elevator because of how old they are. My legs hurt when I got to the top, though. I guess being twelve isn't as young as I thought. But the view was great. Really panoramic and all that stuff.

"I wonder if I spit from up here, if it would kill someone?" I asked Beege.

"The sight of your face might kill someone, but the spit wouldn't, stupid. It would evaporate."

Beege doesn't know very much, but he might be right. I mean, about the spit.

After that, we drove out to Mount Vernon to see George Washington's home. I was excited about going, but I wasn't too excited when we got there. Maybe it was because there were all these people standing in line to get in. Also, my feet were tired. I don't care much about

29

looking at a bunch of furniture in rooms, either. Mom does. She was noticing everything, even stuff like there were no closets anywhere. She said they probably had something like wardrobes, but she didn't see one around.

Migsy noticed something historical and interesting, too. No bathrooms. Not one. I saw some funny-looking pots up this small staircase, and I thought to myself— maybe. But I didn't say anything to Migsy because she always asks these loud questions, and I didn't want to embarrass myself. I read someplace once that people in those days didn't take a lot of baths. I can see why when you think of all the trouble. They probably went around smelling crummy. Even George Washington.

I started getting more interested when we came through the house on the other side and saw stuff like where they kept the horses and carriages. That was pretty neat. Also, I liked the old brick kitchen with the dark wooden bowls all over, and the big old wooden tables and big iron pots. Great big fireplaces, too. I guess if you were a kid then, it would have been fun to mess around in a place like that.

While I'm on the subject of kitchens, I have to tell you about this crazy kitchen in our new house. It looks okay when you're just standing around looking at it. That's all Mom did before we bought the house. But when we started moving into it, were we surprised! There are all these nutty drawers and little cupboards with swinging shelf things inside. It sounds kind of neat when you first think about it, but like Mom said, a teeny, tiny drawer that holds maybe two spoons is great, if you can remember which teeny, tiny drawer the spoons are in when you're in a panic and need them right away.

There are millions of these puny drawers around our kitchen. No big drawers at all. And the swinging stuff is downright dangerous. Mom nearly had her hand smashed to hamburger the day we moved in, when she pulled open this door over the sink and a huge breadboard came roaring down to the counter top. We figured then that some nut must have gotten loose in the kitchen when they were building the place. It took Mom about the whole first day trying to figure out where she was going to put everything.

She made a lot of jokes about it. I guess I believed the jokes, and I was glad that Mom was being herself again and feeling okay. Except for her red, puffy hand, I mean. But once I passed by the kitchen door and saw her leaning on the counter. I think she was crying. It made me scared all over again.

Guys think they should do something when a girl or someone is crying. I do, anyway. You know, stand on your head or something like that. But I never know what to do. I ended up not going in to see Mom. Maybe if I'd been Micky or Beege, I would have. Then it might have helped. It was a good thing there was a lot of stuff I had to do so I couldn't sit around thinking about it.

Most of the day Beege and I spent helping Dad unpack stuff the movers were bringing in. Migsy helped, too, for about five minutes. After she unpacked a couple of things, she started playing with all the papers our junk was wrapped in. Pretty soon she was living in this big cardboard box, having a tea party and all that stuff. I would have clobbered her, but at least she wasn't bothering anyone, so I didn't.

Suddenly, Beege disappeared. I didn't think much

about it at first. Then a long time went by, and he didn't show up.

"Where's Beege?" I finally asked Dad.

"Around somewhere." This was pretty brilliant of Dad, and I told him so. Then Dad told me a couple of things. After that he said, "Well, if you're so anxious about your brother, why don't you go look for him?"

"Okay, I will," I said, and stomped out.

I found Beege in a hurry, because he was just where I thought he would be. A little while before he disappeared, I'd seen him unpack his sports gear and begin tossing his basketball around with this gone look on his face. I remembered that the day we'd bought the house he'd found a basketball net hanging over the garage door. That's where he was, shooting baskets. He didn't pay any attention to me when I appeared.

I decided to open the conversation. "You all through offering your valuable help inside?" I asked him.

"Oh, shut up and go wrinkle a few papers," Beege replied. "I'll be in when I feel like it."

"I'll wait," I said.

"Be my guest," said Beege.

Actually, I like to watch Beege shoot baskets. He moves like this big jungle cat. I would have liked to throw a few balls myself, but I wasn't about to ask, and I knew Beege would never offer. So I just stood around, watching. Beege acted like I wasn't even there.

Then without even turning to look at me, he said, "Wipe that sneer off your face."

I happen to have a crummy mouth that goes up on one side, and sometimes when I'm smiling at someone, it looks like I think they're stupid or something. My smile really does look like a sneer. Even when I'm just standing around with my face doing nothing, it looks like that. Well, I didn't answer Beege, and this made him mad.

"Look, Andrew, wipe it off or I'll belt you one!" He turned and raised the basketball as if he was going to clobber me with it. I turned and ran down the driveway to the front of the house, then around and on down to the other side of the yard. I stood behind this magnolia tree and waited to see if Beege was really after me. He didn't appear, but I didn't feel like going back into the house either. I knew I'd get the word from Dad for ducking out and not showing up again, but then I figured maybe Beege would too if I mentioned that he'd been just goofing around.

I stood behind the tree a while watching the house through the leaves. The movers had already gone, but the front yard was still pretty well littered up with packing junk. I'd about decided maybe I'd go back in, when I noticed this kid standing by the hedge that divides our house from the next one. It was hard to tell how old he was. If he was anywhere near my age, I thought, he was pretty big for it.

The guy kept staring at me, so I kept staring back. I figured if he'd smile at me, I'd smile back. But he didn't. After a couple of minutes, he dug into his pocket and pulled out a pack of gum. I thought maybe he was going to offer me a stick. He didn't. He shook out one stick of gum, slow and careful, partly looking at me and partly at the gum. Then he unwrapped the stick, crumpled up the paper, and threw it toward me. Right by my feet. Right on our lawn. He put the gum in his mouth and started chewing it, kind of rolling it around to one side, sticking his tongue into his cheek and out again, all the time staring at me.

I never did look down at the piece of gum paper at my feet, but I saw it there even while I was staring back at the guy. It was a pretty small piece of paper, but I could see it like it was this big rock. Like someone had thrown this big rock at me. A couple more minutes went by.

Finally, the guy opened his mouth to say something. "Well, aren't you going to pick it up?"

"Pick what up?" I asked.

"You stupid or something?" the guy asked.

"I never noticed," I said.

"You better start noticing a few things. We don't like people in the neighborhood who leave garbage all over their front yard."

I saw then that the guy was standing on our lawn, just over the line. "Well, if *you'd* step off, the place would have a lot less garbage on it," I said. I thought I was pretty brilliant. "Besides, in case you didn't know it, you're trespassing."

He stepped back off the grass onto the sidewalk, and after he looked at me some more as if I had milk whiskers on my face, he drooped his eyelids and gave me this slit-eye stare.

"You military?"

"Maybe."

"Hmmm—transients. Army, I suppose."

I didn't feel like giving this guy the time. But the

way he made *Army* sound kind of dirty made me burn up all of a sudden, and I busted out.

"Air Force, for your information."

"Hmmm," said the guy again. "I guess your dad's a hotshot pilot."

"You must be stupid or something," I said. "Everyone in the Air Force doesn't fly." I don't know why I can't learn to shut up. I knew this guy was giving me the needle, and anything I said, he was going to have something to say back. But I never learn.

"What you mean is that your dad washed out!"

"Oh yeah! He just never wanted to fly." I was lying. It's pretty sad, but Dad did wash out of flight training just before he was going to get his wings. I don't know why, but it's sad. Especially for this big athletic type like my dad. But I wasn't going to tell this big jerk about it. I was sorry I'd told him anything.

"Hmmmph!" he sneered. I could tell he didn't believe me.

"So what does *your* dad do?" I asked, sneering back.

"*My* dad's a lawyer."

I tried to think of something gruesome to say about that. I couldn't. Later I thought that I could have said I supposed he was a *criminal* lawyer who just went around defending people who were guilty as all heck. I always think about these cool insults when it's too late. All I did then was sneer a little more. Like I said, sneering comes pretty easy to me. At least, it does to my face.

Then the guy pointed his thumb over his shoulder and said, "That's *my* house over there."

I should have guessed. All the houses in our neighborhood are these old colonial types like ours, except the house he pointed out. It was so new it hurt, like a pair of new shoes. And it was big. It was too big for the dinky lot. There was a round driveway that went up to the door, and in front of it a patch of ground that was filled up with a bunch of rocks and statues. It looked like a cemetery. I wanted to tell the guy what his house looked like, but it seemed as if he was going to get a little friendly, telling me about his house and all. Instead he got another nasty look on his face.

"We live here permanently, see? And we don't like transients littering up the neighborhood. So you'd better pick up that piece of paper, see?" This sounded pretty stupid, because our whole yard was a mess of papers from the moving stuff, but I knew the piece of paper he meant.

I looked at him and didn't say anything.

"You'd better pick it up if you don't want your block knocked off," he said.

I made a quick mental deduction about the situation. In the first place, I can't fight my way out of a paper sack. In the second place, the guy was a heck of a lot bigger than I was. What I'm trying to say is, I was chicken. I have to admit it. On the other hand, I sure didn't want to pick up the gum wrapper and ruin my reputation forever. The smart thing to do was walk calmly back into the house, only my beautiful, straight-A brain didn't think of that. What I did was to start walking away from the house as fast as I could, on down the street.

"I'll pick it up when I get back," I called over my shoulder.

36

The guy never even tried to follow me. "Where do you think you're going?" he shouted.

"Around," I said.

"Well, I'll be waiting right here for you."

"You'll have a long wait, buddy," I said, but only to myself. I wasn't about to make him change his mind about coming after me.

Anyway, it wasn't until I'd turned the corner, out of sight of our house, that I remembered I didn't have one crummy idea about where I was going to go. So I slowed down, deciding I'd just have to wander around loose for a while. I was worried about getting back to help Dad, but I didn't know how I'd get back into the house without the guy seeing me, and I sure wasn't going through that chewing-gum-wrapper scene again. One way or another, I was going to have to kill a little time.

Just around the block from our house, I walked past this girl who was trimming branches from the hedge in front of her house. I thought it was a weird thing for a girl to be doing. She was pretty nice looking, too. She had these huge green eyes and long, straight brown hair that kind of hung around her shoulders. I wasn't staring or anything. You just couldn't help noticing. She saw me, too, and gave me this big smile.

"Hi," she said.

"Hi," I said.

"You're new here, aren't you?" she asked me.

"Yeah," I said.

"Are you the people who just bought the house around the corner?" she asked.

"Yeah," I said.

"I'm glad someone finally bought it. I like that house," she said.

"Yeah," I said.

After that, I ran out of anything else to say, so I started shuffling off.

"Hey," the girl said, "my name's Sally—Sally Ardery. What's yours?"

"Uh—Andrew," I said.

"Welcome to the neighborhood, Andrew."

I had this terrible feeling that I was turning pink, so I started moving away faster.

"See you around," Sally said.

"Yeah," I said. I'm this great conversationalist when I meet a girl. You may have noticed. Anyway, it was nice to meet someone whose big object in life wasn't throwing chewing-gum wrappers around.

I wandered off a couple more blocks, and then I decided to sit down somewhere and rest my old flat feet. At that moment I happened to be passing a tall, spiked iron fence. The bars were set into a low cement wall which I figured would be okay to sit on even if it only stuck out about two inches. I sat down and braced myself on the sidewalk to keep my bottom from sliding off. About five minutes of this was all I could take, though, because I got pretty numb in the rear. But as I was getting ready to move on, something made me turn and look through the fence.

There were these big bushes on the other side of the fence, but not so big or so thick that I couldn't see through them. Someone was walking down a path on the other side of the bushes. It was a lady, and she was walking very slowly, looking around and smiling. To herself, I guess, because she was all alone.

This was about the smallest lady I'd ever seen in my life. She looked as if she practically didn't come any higher than my belly button. I don't mean that she was really just a little girl. In fact, she looked pretty old. Her hair was almost all gray, and it was pulled back tight from her face into a kind of knot on her neck. But she didn't walk like she was old. Her back was as straight as if she had an iron rod through it.

I noticed her dress, too. It had a high collar, like a minister's collar, only higher, and it fitted up tight around her neck. The rest of the dress was like a tube, straight up and down, and long to the ground. It was a shiny, light green color. I don't know why I remember so much except that the lady was like part of the garden. There was something else, too. She was Chinese. I guess I didn't expect to see a Chinese lady in that garden.

I stood and gawked through the fence, peeking around the bushes. I felt crummy, spying like that, but I went on doing it anyway. As the lady walked along, I sneaked on down the fence, watching her. Pretty soon I came to a big gate. That was where I saw her turn off and go toward what I guessed was the house. After that, I couldn't see her anymore. But right in front of my nose, to the side of the gate, was a bronze plate with words on it. The words were in big printed letters, and they said "Robert E. Lee." Under that there was a lot of Chinese writing.

Robert E. Lee? Chinese writing? Wow! I said to

myself. This house probably once belonged to Robert E. Lee. I mean, he lived in Alexandria, didn't he? Heck, we sat right in his pew in church. Okay, supposing he had these Chinese slaves. Nobody ever said he didn't, did they? Well then, supposing he married one of these slaves, or something like that. Couldn't this old lady in the garden just possibly be a real live Chinese descendant of Robert E. Lee?

Shut up, I told myself. I don't want to hear any more about it. So just shut up.

I started to walk away from the gate to stop thinking about it, but then I had to turn and look at it one more time. That did it.

Look, I started in again to myself, you don't have to tell anyone about it. You don't have to do anything about it. Just keep it in the back of your head, and one of these days you can come back and sort of look around a little. What harm could there be in that?

In reply, I shrugged my shoulders, stuck my hands in my pockets, and went on staring at the gate. I didn't have to say anything more. I'd already convinced myself that I'd be back.

In the meantime, though, I had a bigger worry, and that was getting home. Had I stayed out long enough to make the guy give up on me and leave, or should I stay longer and have to worry about facing Dad? I decided I was already late, Dad would be mad anyway, so I might as well stay out longer. I hung around the fence some more, having further thoughts about Robert E. Lee's Chinese descendants. After I'd killed about half an hour, I went home.

The guy was gone, but the chewing-gum wrapper wasn't. I hate to tell you what I did next, but I went over and picked it up. After that, I went in the house.

Dad really pinned my ears back, asking me what did I mean disappearing for so long, telling me what a goof-off I was, and asking me what was the big idea when Mom was sick and we all had to work to help out. While Dad was giving it to me, Beege walked in.

"And where were *you?*" Dad asked, ready to light into him, too.

"Out at the garage," said Beege.

"Oh," said Dad. "Well, I guess there's work to be done there, too. But maybe you'd better stick around here, Beege, because we still have a lot of unpacking to do." Period. That was all Beege got.

I stood there like a big jerk and didn't say anything about Beege playing basketball. I just kept my mouth shut, and Beege never even looked at me. Or said thanks. Or anything. I knew he never would.

Four

For a few days, things seemed to get a whole lot better. Beege quit bugging me so much, for one thing. Maybe because he was feeling pretty good. You see, he'd met this guy down at the music shop near us one day when he was buying himself some new guitar strings. Beege meets people like that, real easy. Anyway, Beege was telling him about this bunch of guys he played guitar with in California, and also how he gave lessons. Next thing, the guy invited him over to meet his friends, and then right after that, Beege was lined up to give lessons to some girls. It doesn't take him five minutes to become the big deal.

Migsy was doing all right, too. She liked her new room, and she spent a lot of time visiting Glorious in the backyard. I helped her clean out the pond. It looked pretty good, and we had big plans for maybe building a waterfall for him the next summer. Migsy got herself a friend right away, too. I didn't approve much of the friend. Her name was Diane Kogel. She turned out to be the kid sister of the guy with the chewing-gum-wrapper disposal problem. I found out his name was Arthur.

Dad started work right away. He liked his job and he liked his boss, so he was feeling pretty good along with everyone else. But the best thing was Mom. I guess being settled in a house was a good thing for her even if it wasn't the house of her dreams, as she said. Also, the weather turned great, and Dad was able to get off work a little early to take her to play some golf. Mom is this great athlete like the rest of the family. She used to be a big tennis champion in school, and golf later on. I don't understand anybody getting all excited about chasing this little white ball around with a club, but it did something for Mom. She was singing all over the place and really meaning it for a change. I stopped worrying about her so much.

I made out okay. I got my room settled and started digging in, with old Grover helping me out. We got him the day after we moved in. It really felt good to flop down on my window seat and have the Grove flopped down beside me. Grover is pretty much my dog. I feed him, anyway. I have to admit that dogs like me. It's better than nothing. A whole lot better. I like dogs.

I was doing some worrying about starting school, though. I always worry about starting school, even when I know the school I'm going to. Also, I was worrying about a paper route. I personally have never had a paper route, but I really wanted one. To earn some money. Part of it was for college, but most of it was for this new bicycle. A bicycle doesn't sound like a very big deal for a twelve-year-old guy, but it *is* a big deal when your bike is about a jillion years old and got handed down to you from an older brother who got it handed down to him from another brother. My bicycle's dents had dents, for Pete's sake. Riding around on it was downright dangerous. I mean, to the general public as well as myself. So for me, a bicycle was a big deal. I wanted a three-speed English racer, but I'd settle for anything. I wished I could get rich giving a few crummy guitar lessons to a couple of crummy girls.

I didn't see Arthur Kogel again for a couple of days. I don't know if he ever came around to check on the chewing-gum wrapper. His sister Diane, though, *she* hung around all the time I was cleaning up the front yard by order of Dad. Asking me a bunch of stupid questions. What a pest! I finally got rid of her by telling Migsy I'd clobber her if she didn't get Diane out of my hair, which Migsy kindly did.

Anyway, on the last day before school started, I figured I ought to get some of my odd jobs wound up. A big one was to scrape the rust off my bike. Migsy came out to the backyard to watch.

Pretty soon she started wearing her thinking look. "Do we get snow and things like that around here?"

"Sure we do. Ice and snow and just about everything," I answered.

Migsy got up from where she was sitting on the

ground and walked over to the pond. Then she stared a while at the water with this big thinky look on her face. I went on scraping rust.

"What's Glorious going to do?" she asked after a long while.

"Do about what?"

"The ice and snow and cold. What's he going to do? He doesn't have a frog house to go into, and he doesn't have a fur coat like Grover."

Migsy reasons pretty good for a little kid, even if some of it comes out weird. I right away had this vision of Glorious sitting in front of his frog mansion with a mink cape around his neck. I decided, however, that I wouldn't give Migsy the business about this.

"Look, Migsy, frogs hibernate," I said.

"What's that?"

"It's when these animals like frogs and turtles dig into places and stay there, not eating or anything, until it gets warm again."

"What's Glorious going to dig into?" Migsy went on. "The pond is made of cement, isn't it?"

Like I said, Migsy reasons pretty good for a kid.

"Maybe he jumps out of the pond and goes away someplace."

"Is that what he did last year? Where did he go *last* year?"

"Sheesh, Migsy, how should I know what he did last year? You want me to ask him if I can read his diary or something? I'm not a crummy frog mind reader, for Pete's sake." I gave my bike a good swipe with the steel wool and scraped a big hunk of myself off along with the rust. It never pays to get mad when you're doing something, I've found out. And I was getting mad, because I was suddenly beginning to worry about this stupid frog.

"Well, you can try to think of something. You don't have to be so dumb!" said Migsy, beginning to blubber.

"I *am* thinking, for your information," I said. "In fact, I've just thought of something."

"What?" sniffed Migsy.

"I'm going to—I'm going to—call the Smithsonian!" Actually, I'd just thought of it practically at the moment I said it. Once in a while I get these brilliant flashes.

"What can they do?" Migsy asked.

"Oh, they know all about animals. They stuff them and all that."

"You're not going to have Glorious stuffed! That's murder!" said Migsy, dripping again.

"Look, Migsy, I'm not going to have them *do* anything. I'll just ask them to tell us what to do, like how to store Glorious over the winter. I'll call the reptile department at the zoo. The zoo is part of the Smithsonian, too, you know." Migsy kindly began to look impressed at this. I thought I was displaying quite a lot of brilliance myself.

"Call them right now. Right now!" she said, jumping up and down.

"Okay, I will." I went into the house.

It was pretty hard to find the number to call. I looked under *Zoo*. Then I looked under *Smithsonian*. I even looked for *Frog* in the yellow pages. Then I decided to ask Mom.

"You might try information," she said. "But first, just for laughs, why don't you look it up under *United States Government?*"

"You mean they have a department in the government just for frogs?" I said.

"Don't squeak, Andrew," said Mom. "And what you do is *first* look up the *United States Government*. Then you find *Smithsonian Institution* under that. Then look under the subtitles until you find something that looks like *Zoo*."

I did this. You know, Mom hit it right. Pneumonia sure doesn't affect the brain. *National Zoological Park* is what it said under *Smithsonian Institution*. Man, was I excited! Yours truly, Andrew, telephoning the Smithsonian.

The guy I got at the reptile department of the zoo told me all about what to do with Glorious. Migsy was right. He wouldn't hibernate in cement. And he would probably go off looking for some good mud someplace and never show up again. Pretty ungrateful, but you've got to face it, a frog doesn't have much loyalty. So this meant, the guy told me, we'd have to bring him inside and keep him in water. And feed him bugs and stuff like mealworms. He said you could buy mealworms in a pet shop.

Migsy was all excited about this and thought we should bring Glorious right into the basement and fix him his indoor pool in case it snowed the next day. It was eighty-five degrees out at the moment. I informed her of this fact, but she was still sure we should have some mealworms right away just in case. So I said I'd go. I knew there was this pet store in the shopping center near us, and Mom said it was okay for me to go if I came right back. I wondered where in heck I could go with a bunch of mealworms.

Anyway, I got my rusty, trusty bike up on its wheels and moved it out to the front yard. I have to admit it looked just as miserable as ever, even with all my hard work and losing half my skin and all that. But anything is better than walking.

And who do you think should be standing right out on the sidewalk in front of our house? No less than my old friend, Arthur Kogel.

"Nice-looking contraption you've got there. Where'd you get it?" he said with this friendly sneer on his face. Then he reached down and picked a piece of our grass and started chewing on it.

"Shut up," I said politely, under my breath.

"You deaf? I said where'd you get the wreck?"

I had forgotten to pull up my kickstand in the backyard, and I knew I had to do it before I could ride away. Naturally, it stuck, so I had to stand there on the driveway trying to get the thing up and get *myself* stuck in a crummy conversation with A. Kogel.

"None of your business," I said.

"What's wrong? Can't your dad afford to buy you a new one?" He spit out the piece of grass he was chewing, right back on our lawn. I decided to ignore it, because I didn't want to get back into the garbage collection business again.

"He can afford anything he wants to."

"Yeah? Then why'd he buy this old lemon of a house? You really got taken."

"It so happens that we like this house, friend. And so do some other people. Uh, Sally—Sally Ardery thinks it's a great house."

Suddenly a big surprised look came over Arthur's face. Then he raised his eyebrows and stared at me, very heavy lidded and suspicious.

"How do you know her?" he asked. The way he said "her" made it sound as if I'd mentioned someone I wasn't supposed to have the nerve to know.

"Oh, I get around," I said.

He stood there looking as if he was doing some big thinking. Then he gave me this nasty kind of sniff.

"Hmmmph! What does she know, anyway? She's got a crazy mother."

"What is that supposed to mean?" I asked.

"Oh, you'll find out," he said.

I wasn't going to lower myself by getting all curious and asking a bunch of questions that he probably wouldn't answer anyway, so I kept my mouth shut for a change. At any rate, the kickstand suddenly came up with a big jerk and nearly knocked me over.

"Ha, ha, ha," said Arthur, grabbing his stomach like it was aching with merriment. "Here, maybe your dad would like to borrow some of this to get you a decent vehicle." He pulled out a wallet from his back pocket and then pulled a bunch of paper money and waved it at me.

I sure wanted to smash his face in, making cracks about Dad. With Dad not flying and not getting flight pay and having four kids and all, we're not exactly billionaires. But we're not exactly poverty-stricken either. So what if I had a rusty bicycle? I tell you, I sure did want to smash his face in, waving all that lousy money around in my face.

I started off as fast as I could, which wasn't very fast.

I was wobbling all over the place, and the back wheel was squeaking its crummy self to pieces.

Arthur started singing "Off We Go Into the Wild Blue Yonder" in time to the squeak. I tell you, it's a good thing I got away as fast as I did, or I don't know what I would have done to him.

The next morning I woke up with a queer feeling in my stomach. I didn't worry about it, though, because I'd had the feeling before and I knew what it was.

The feeling wasn't because of what happened with Arthur Kogel. It wasn't because of those crazy, mixed-up mealworms either—though they're enough to make you sick. They crawl around in this kind of sawdusty stuff in a little plastic bag, very delicious and appetizing. Yecch! Migsy and I thought we should try a couple of them out on Glorious to see if he liked the menu.

"Hi, Henry, old boy," I said to this worm I pulled out of the bag. "Glorious, I would like to introduce you to your next meal, Henry M. Worm." I laid Henry carefully on a leaf so Glorious could get at him.

Migsy grabbed Henry up. "You can't do that," she screamed. "You can't name a worm. Now he's a pet. You can't feed someone a pet. You're stupid, Andrew."

Migsy was right. I don't mean about my being stupid, but about not naming stuff. I should have known better. I moved my face close to the worm so that we were practically nose to nose. "My humble apologies," I said to him. "I thought you were someone I knew. Migsy, I swear I've never seen this worm before in my life." Then I took the worm from her and put him back on the leaf.

Glorious just sat looking straight ahead like he never saw that worm. But he saw him all right. Kerchunk, right down the gullet. What a trapper! Migsy wanted to feed him the whole bag right away, but I wouldn't let her. I wasn't about to have to go to the pet shop every day for this guy's groceries.

Anyway, about the queer feeling in my stomach. That was because it was the first day of school. You'd think a person would get over it by the time he gets to the seventh grade.

Also, you'd think with all the millions of first days of school in our family, everything would run smooth as glass. It never has. Mom starts bugging us at least a whole day before about getting our clothes together and all that boloney, but something always gets fouled up. On the day I'm talking about, Beege ended up all out of clean shorts. When anything like this happens, someone always starts yelling around at someone else to find out whose fault it is.

"See here, Beege," Dad said, "your mother asked you kids to see that you were all set for school this morning. Especially you two older ones. It seems to me that providing yourself with a clean pair of shorts isn't asking too much of a sixteen-year-old boy."

This was all going on in the kitchen where Mom was fixing breakfast. She put down the orange juice pitcher and turned around. Her eyes looked a little funny, I thought. For a change, I was all dressed and sitting at the breakfast table.

"Bill, this isn't Beege's fault," Mom said. "I should have checked their things over. Laundry isn't their responsibility." She turned back to the counter and brushed her hair away from her forehead in a kind of tired way.

"Maybe not as a general rule," Dad said, "but Beege should have used a little sense of responsibility and judgment. These seem to be two commodities that are sadly lacking around here. Beege, you'll just have to run down to the laundry basket and fish yourself out some dirty underwear. Or, if that's going to offend your dignity, borrow a pair of mine."

Beege looked sulky. "Yours are too big."

"How about trying a safety pin?" I offered. My tone of voice was all bright and shiny, but not exactly helpful, if you know what I mean.

"Shut up, Andrew. Keep your big nose out of my business."

"That's enough, Beege," Dad said. Then he looked kind of anxiously toward Mom. "Just get moving. Dirty underwear or borrow mine. Suit yourself. But get on with it."

Maybe I shouldn't say this, but I got a huge, overgrown charge from seeing Beege get chewed out. I wasn't exactly feeling sorry for him and his big, fat underwear problem. I knew that once he got started in school and was right away a famous basketball hero, he'd start getting treated like this precious jewel wrapped up in cotton. No matter what he does, he always ends up being the big deal.

Beege left and then Migsy walked in. "Mommy, help me button up the back of my dress," she said.

"Here, let me do it, Piglet," Dad said.

"No! No!" Mom turned from the counter again. "I've got to do *something* right around here."

I saw Dad's eyebrows go up a fraction. Then he looked toward me. I don't know why. I just shrugged my shoulders, because I didn't know what I was supposed to do. Then Dad turned back down to the newspaper, but I could see that his face looked worried.

Mom had buttoned about two buttons on Migsy's dress, when suddenly she cried out, "Oh no!"

"What's wrong?" Dad asked, real quick.

"Oh, this button came off!" Mom threw her head down on the counter and busted out into these awful sobs.

Mom'd gotten upset lots of times before. But this was different. I can't describe very well how different it was. I mean, to get all sobby and hysterical about a lousy button coming off. It was spooky and terrible.

Dad jumped right up and put his arms around her. After that, he made her go upstairs and lie down. She put up an argument, but he made her do it. Dad said we'd manage okay. So she went up to their room, and we managed. It was a sad breakfast in more ways than one. When I left for school that morning, my stomach was feeling a lot worse than usual for the first day of school.

Five

Migsy's school is right up the street from us, which is great for her, and it meant Mom didn't have to worry about Migs crossing a whole bunch of streets to get there. It was good to have one thing Mom didn't have to worry about. But Beege and I have to take the bus. We go to different schools—Beege goes to high school and I go to junior high—but we take the same bus. He gets off before I do, though.

Beege was pretty decent walking to the bus with me. He talked to me and we kind of kidded around. But after we got to the bus, he saw a couple of the guys he'd met before and also this girl, and he moved away from me like I was a poisoned grape.

Arthur Kogel was at the bus. I figured he would be.

He was busy talking to this other guy, but every so often they'd both look over at me. It didn't make my stomach feel any better.

Sally Ardery was waiting for the bus, too. She was standing with a bunch of girls, all gabbing away. She saw me and stopped talking long enough to give me a big smile. I guess I smiled back, and then I looked down and started reading an old matchbook cover that was on the sidewalk. It was advertising a place called Harvey's Grill. I get a lot of information reading stuff like that.

Sally didn't come over to talk to me. A kid never does leave a bunch of kids to come over and talk to you if you're all alone. Especially if you're not the big deal. I don't mean that Sally isn't neat. She is, but she can't help it if she's a kid. I wouldn't leave a bunch of kids either to go talk to some crummy guy standing all alone.

I didn't sit alone on the bus, though. This high school guy sat with me, but he never said anything to me and kept his nose stuck in a book until he got off. Still, I wasn't alone on the seat.

Everyone says there is this great big change when you go into seventh grade. You could fool me. It's still school any way you look at it. One thing, though, you don't stay in the same room all day. You do stay with the same kids except for this one elective course you get to take, but you don't wear out your bottom in the same old desk. You go to a different room and have a different teacher for every subject.

My science and math teachers are neat. They're men, Mr. Neilsen and Mr. Ewell. My English teacher is Mrs. Carmichael. Her first name is Beverly. I found that out right away. Her hair is blonde, and she's kind of young. I wish I had her for my homeroom. I don't. What I have is Mrs. Rasmussen.

Mrs. Rasmussen also teaches social studies. I personally think her hair is too dark for the way her face looks. Also, she wears this same old dress almost every day. It's kind of a long green sweater. Maybe it's a sweater that stretched or something. It's pretty gruesome. Mrs. Carmichael would probably look cool in it, but Mrs. Rasmussen just looks like a bone with these weird lumps all over it. I mostly stare at a huge silver butterfly she wears hanging on this green dress between her neck and her stomach. I sort of hypnotize myself watching it dangle around. I've discovered you can do all kinds of interesting things like this to pass time.

After I got over having Mrs. Rasmussen for my homeroom teacher the first day of school, I looked around at the rest of the kids. Naturally, being new, I didn't know anyone. That is until just before the bell rang, when in walked Arthur Kogel and this guy he'd been with on the bus. The guy was so big he made Arthur look like Tom Thumb. My insides climbed into an elevator and went down fast. Arthur was bad enough by himself, but with a character like that to back him up, I figured you could count the days I had left on the fingers of half a hand. Up until I saw Arthur and this buddy of his, whose name turned out to be Melvin Funkhauser, I never thought a twelve-year-old guy needed a will.

The rest of it was about the way it always is. Most of the time at school during lunch periods and any other free times, I kind of goof around by myself. I'm not saying I especially like being a loner, but that's the way it is. The first day of school there are probably a lot of other people goofing around by themselves, but if you ever go up and talk to a guy who looks like he's by himself, he turns out to be the most popular guy in class, and he's just waiting around for a friend. It kills me the way I always pick out the wrong guy to talk to. Other kids must be greased the way they slide around making a buddy or getting in with a bunch of kids. I swear it. I never see it happen, but suddenly there's everyone all set up and I'm still by my crummy self.

Some of this is probably because of this business of physical education, after several periods of which I turn out to be about as popular as four hours of math homework. I mean, when you send a ball to me, it's like sending it to a big hunk of Swiss cheese, only I'm all holes and no ·cheese. The ball goes right through me every time. Who wants anything to do with a big deal like that?

Also there's my other problem about being smart in school. I just can't learn to keep my big mouth shut. I mean, supposing the teacher is showing a filmstrip on something like religious idols. Some kid is mumbling around trying to talk about it, but he can't think of the right word. "Deification," I blast out. Everyone turns to look at me, and the teacher gives me a huge smile and says, "Very good, Andrew." All kinds of these miserable-type words are lying around in my head. Infinitesimal. Pacifistic. Stuff like that. And all this other miscellaneous information too.

I always say to myself, "Shut up, Andrew. Just shut up." Then my mind goes blank, and I hear this voice giving out with some learned piece of information. It's my voice, naturally, and the next thing you know there's the teacher saying, "Very good, Andrew."

I wasn't in the class very long before I noticed that when this kind of stuff happened, a couple of kids would look at me as if I was a pile of eraser droppings on the floor, and then they'd give a raised-eyebrow look to their buddies. This kind of performance was pretty noticeable with Arthur and Melvin. Soon they started doing things that were pretty noticeable with *me*, stuff like edging up to me in the halls and accidentally socking me in the ribs. It's a good thing that only Grover watches me undress at night or there'd have been a lot of explaining to do about the black-and-blue polka dots all over me.

I used to explain to someone about this kind of stuff when I was a little guy, but Micky or Beege or even Dad would always say, "Well, why didn't you sock him back?" Then Dad would tell Micky or Beege to give me a boxing lesson, and if they did, the lesson would last about two and a half minutes. I guess I must have been pretty hopeless the way they just gave up. I'd end up going to my room to bawl, not because I got hit in the first place, but because I wasn't the big deal with Micky and Beege. So I quit showing off my crummy wounds.

Anyway, I pretty well convinced myself that Arthur and Melvin were going to be satisfied with this minor kind of activity. They never jumped me from behind a bush to rough me up or anything like that, and outside of hallway maneuvers and using me for a soccer ball in phys. ed. when the coach wasn't looking, they pretty much left me alone. So I quit worrying about them and went around with my big fat head in a sack.

Dad came home one evening and told us that he was going to get this medal for the work he'd done in California. The Commendation Medal is a pretty big deal even though Dad didn't make out that it was anything. I knew he was proud, though, and we were all pretty excited. You just never figure your dad for a medal, especially if he doesn't fly and will probably be warming a desk chair for the rest of his life. He told us that we were all invited to the Pentagon for the presentation ceremony.

"Oh boy!" Migsy said. "We get a whole morning off from school."

"Nothing doing," I told her. "The ceremony isn't until eleven-thirty. I bet we have to go to school, and then Mom will pick us up in time to get to the Pentagon." I was right, even though I hoped I wasn't up until the last minute.

We had to take notes to school asking permission to be excused, and when I handed mine to Mrs. Rasmussen, she read it and then gave me this little smirky look like we were sharing some big secret. It was embarrassing as all heck, but at least she kept her mouth shut about what was in the note.

The worst thing about having to go to school before the ceremony was that we had to get all dressed up before we left home. It's okay to be wearing a coat and tie and all that when the rest of the guys are too, like if there's a school program or something. Otherwise you feel like this big ape.

I had to put on my good blue suit. Well, it *was* good when Micky had it. Also Beege. I guess it's still okay. I'm just sick of looking at it hanging around in everybody's closet. Now even I'm beginning to grow out of it.

After the jacket sleeves end, there's about an inch of my bare wrists flapping in the wind.

"Andrew," Mom said with this huge sigh as I was leaving for school, "we must do something about a suit for you when we—oh dear—I guess when *I* can get around to it." She had that worried, gone kind of look on her face that I was getting pretty used to seeing by that time. Then she put some spit on her finger and tried to push down a piece of my hair with it.

Someone is always trying to push down my hair with spit. It doesn't do any good. My hair grows in directions a compass never heard of. All I end up with after all this attention is no results and a head covered with spit. I wish people would wise up.

Anyway, right after the bell rang at school, Mrs. Rasmussen looked toward me with her smirky look. I ducked way down in my seat. Mrs. Rasmussen has this very skinny nose that opens up big at the end and starts to quiver when she's going to make some important announcement. Then she prunes up her mouth and snorts. She should have been a horse. I had a feeling that something terrible was going to happen to me. I turned and stared out the window so I wouldn't be caught looking at her. I was wasting my valuable time.

"Andrew," she said, "wouldn't you like to stand up and tell the class what special event is going to happen in your family today? I'm sure the class would be thrilled to know where you're going and what is going to happen there."

I rose. I swear I could feel my wrists growing out of my sleeves a mile a minute. Also, I knew I was turning my usual lousy shade of red. I stood. Then I stood some more.

"Come, come, Andrew, don't be bashful. We know you have a voice."

After that I said a word. I think it was something like "Punagon," but I wouldn't swear it. There must be a million kids in that school whose Dads have gotten medals, this being a big military area and all. I felt like yelling out, "Why are you picking on me, you big horse!"

Mrs. Rasmussen gave another snort and busted out into this horsey grin. "Well, Andrew, I suppose I'll have to speak for you. Class, Andrew's father is being presented with a medal for heroism at the Pentagon today. I'm sure we're all very proud for Andrew, aren't we!"

As usual, I should have kept my big mouth shut. I mean, so who'd know the difference about why my dad was getting a medal? "Snot herism," I mumbled into space. "Sfer sm stuff he did in thoffice 'n California."

A couple of people snickered, and Arthur Kogel let out this big snort. I began to feel like I was coming down with a pretty good case of the rigor mortis, so I started to sit down before I fell down dead.

"Just a minute, Andrew," said Mrs. Rasmussen. "Class, I think we should all give Andrew a big hand!" Then she started clapping, and the class started clapping too, except that the class also threw in a few catcalls and boos and hisses. Also a large bunch of snickers.

I'm just an ordinary guy. I don't understand why something like that should happen to me. I wanted to kill Mrs. Rasmussen, but how can you go around killing someone who thinks she's doing you this big favor?

I went on dying in my seat until the bell rang, and then I had to listen to a bunch of hilarious jokes all the way to math. I guess I should have remembered then to detour through the boys' room, because Mom had told us she didn't want to go dragging us all to a bathroom at the Pentagon. But with trying to get away from all the funny people and trying to get to my desk as fast as I could get there, I forgot all about it. I remembered about ten minutes before math class was over. I can hold out pretty good most of the time, but I decided I'd better not chance it. Mom was going to pick me up right after math, and I wouldn't have time to stop off then. So I got myself excused.

A school hallway during classes is weird, kind of lonely and empty. This is funny because there are all these people right on the other side of the walls. The boys' room is the same way. I guess the girls' room must be too, but I wouldn't know because I personally have never been there. I don't usually like to go to the boys' room during class because of the queer hollow sound. And then I always get this kind of shock when I suddenly see myself in the big mirror. I especially didn't want to see myself in the mirror that day.

Anyway, I didn't have to wait for a cubicle because during class they're all empty. In grade school they didn't have doors on the cubicles, but they do in this school. I guess it's okay, in case you'd ever need to throw up or something. I went in the farthest one against the wall and closed the door.

I guess I wasn't in there two minutes when I looked down under the door and saw this pair of feet. At first I didn't think much about it because I figured here was a guy waiting to get into my cubicle. Then I thought some more. What was a guy waiting to get into my cubicle for when there were about ten empty ones all in a row next to mine? Maybe this guy had a favorite one, I told myself—mine. But then right away I figured who ever heard of a guy having a favorite toilet, for Pete's sake? I took a closer look at this guy's feet. Suddenly I had it figured out.

There is one guy in our class who has the biggest feet in the whole world. The guy is Melvin Funkhauser. Also, he always wears these bright socks, pink and green. You can't miss them. The feet outside my cubicle belonged to Melvin. I decided to finish up my business and get out of there in a hurry. Anyway, like I told myself, if a guy wants to get into your cubicle, you sure as heck don't want to keep him waiting.

Then I noticed another queer thing. Melvin's feet were pointing away from me. One thing I've noticed is that when feet are waiting to get into a cubicle, they're usually pointing toward it. I don't know where I got all the sudden knowledge like I was this Sherlock Holmes of the bathroom, but when the enemy is standing outside your cubicle, you suddenly know all this stuff. I mean, I knew that Melvin's feet weren't waiting to get into the cubicle. They were guarding it.

It didn't take me long to figure that since I might have some trouble getting out the usual way, I'd better try something different. Cubicle walls, except the end one, don't come down to the floor. I guess this is pretty public knowledge. What I decided to do was to get down on my stomach and crawl under the wall to my right. But when I got down, I saw another pair of feet also looking as if they were guarding my cubicle. It didn't take any brains to figure that these belonged to Arthur Kogel. That was it, my escape passage cut off. The wall to my left was the end wall, solid right down to the ground, and I didn't happen to have any dynamite on me. I was really stuck. I couldn't guess how these guys got excused from class, because teachers don't usually let you out ten minutes before the bell unless you're sick or have some big deal going like me. It didn't matter much, because there they were.

I decided then that the only thing for me to do was to pretend I hadn't seen anyone, and just walk out. I started to whistle and push open the door. The feet turned around, and a big hand came smacking down against the door, holding it tight shut.

"Look, Funkhauser, quit monkeying around," I said. "My mom is picking me up and I've got to get out of here."

"Listen to that. Hey, did you hear that, Arthur? Little Cornflakes Kellogg has to get out because his mommy is coming for him. Isn't that sweet? Listen, creep," Melvin said to me, "you'll have to find another way out, because you're not getting out this way!"

I decided then that I'd have to try the stomach route, so I got down and started to crawl under the wall. Splat! It felt like a gallon of water landed on my head.

"You better cut that out, Kogel," I hollered, pulling back into the cubicle.

"Try and make me!" said Arthur.

I was getting pretty mad then. Those dirty crumbs!

Without much thinking, I got back down and started sneaking under the wall again. Splat! More water came down on my head and over my shoulders. I pulled back in.

"Nice try, Cornflakes," Arthur shouted, hooting with laughter. "Hey, Melvin, wasn't that a nice try? Say, class, let's give a big round of applause to old Corny for that nice try." Arthur and Melvin started clapping and hooting their heads off.

"You guys better let me out of here!" I shouted. My voice kind of squeaked off, and it sounded almost like I was starting to cry. But I wasn't. I swear it.

"Hey, would you listen to that?" Melvin said. "The little creep is starting to blubber. Hey, I wonder what his big hero daddy would think about that? Throw the boy a couple of hankies, Arthur."

A few seconds after that, a shower of toilet-paper pieces came floating over the top of the cubicle. They stuck on my wet hair. I started to pull the stuff off and at the same time did some thinking. Maybe I'd better try to stay cool and pleasant, I told myself. It sure wasn't doing me any good to get mad.

"Look, guys, I've just got to get outside. Come on now."

"Aw, he's got to get outside. Now let's figure a good way for Cornflakes to get outside, Melvin. Hey, I have it! I just remembered a good way to get rid of garbage. Flush! Look, Cornflakes, first you pretend you're this goldfish, see?"

"You're a genius, Arthur," Melvin hollered. "Hey, Cornflakes, isn't Arthur a genius?"

I didn't say anything.

Melvin started to rattle the door.

"Yeah, he's a genius," I said.

"Do you know why he's a genius, Cornflakes?"

"No."

"He's a genius because he says you should pretend you're a goldfish and flush yourself down the toilet. Maybe you'll come out somewhere on the good old Potomac, and your mommy can pick you up down there. We'll let her know where you are, Cornflakes. You don't have to worry about a thing."

I couldn't think of anything to say back to this, but I was pretty worried. I mean, all this business about being a goldfish. Supposing they decided to put my head in the toilet and then flush it. I knew I was too big to go down the drain or anything lame-brained like that, but a guy's head can get pretty wet in a situation like that. Maybe even drowned. I didn't think they'd really do it, but you never know.

I was worried about Mom, too. I didn't want to keep her waiting around and then have to answer a lot of questions. More than that, though, I didn't want to get her all shook up. Before this, when one of us kids was late or something like that, she would just get mad, but not shook up. It was different somehow. And even though I kept telling myself that Mom was getting more like she used to be, she really wasn't. I was just lying to myself.

Worrying about her made me start to get mad again. You know, when you get really mad, sometimes you forget to be scared. I don't forget very often, I have to admit it, but I did then.

"Look here, *Fink*hauser!" I shouted.

"What was that you said?" said Melvin. "What was that again, creep?"

"*FINKHAUSER!*" I informed him.

"Hey, Melvin, you going to let the creep get away with that?" Arthur said.

Right then my cubicle door flew back at me. I almost fell into the toilet. Then Melvin came at me, and I thought he was going to push me in. Instead, he grabbed me by the tie. Arthur was standing behind him.

"Listen, if you know what's good for you, you'll get down on your knees and say, 'I am a creep, and I apologize.'" Melvin shook me a couple of times and started to shove me down.

The school bell rang just then.

I don't believe in miracles. I have to be honest. But a school bell is practically a miracle. At least it's saved the lives of a lot of guys, and it sure saved mine. I knew that in a few seconds the boys' room was going to be filled with guys, and I didn't think these two bullies would get caught standing around making my life miserable. So I put up a little resistance to going down. Melvin and Arthur looked at each other.

"Better let him go," Arthur said.

"*This* time," Melvin said, giving me an extra shake with my tie. He nearly knocked my head off. Then he stepped out of the cubicle, and I pushed out after him as fast as I could.

Just as I shoved through the door, I saw Melvin wink at Arthur, and at the same time I felt his big fat foot catch me at the shin. I wheeled out forward, landing hard on my knees and then jolting forward again and hitting the top of my head on the washbowl in front of me. My knees felt as if someone had smashed them with a hammer and knocked them clean up into my legs, and my head felt as if it had gone down to meet them. I guess nothing ever hurt so much in my whole life.

But they weren't through with me yet. Melvin quickly turned on the faucets in a washbasin and started throwing water on me. Arthur joined him, and they both were hooting and hollering and telling me it would make me feel better. They stopped, though, and pretended to be washing their hands the minute the first guy walked in.

I was pretty dizzy, but I got up off my knees. Other guys started coming in, and they all stared at me. I didn't stare back. I just pretended to be straightening out my trousers, and staggered out.

Six

I MANAGED to make it to the street all right, but it was a good thing Mom was a few minutes late. It gave my knees time to stop hurting, so I could stand up straight. I had trouble puckering up my mouth, but I even managed to whistle while I was climbing into the back seat of the car. Mom had already picked up Beege and Migsy. Beege was in back, and Migs was up front with Mom. I guess Mom didn't look real closely at me when she drove up, and she was doing something to the lock on the glove compartment when I got in, so she didn't notice the wet mess. I squeezed down tight into my corner of the car and pretended to get interested in the scenery right away. I figured Beege wouldn't pay much attention to me.

But about thirty seconds later, I felt Beege's eyes examining me. You can tell these types of things even when you're not looking at someone. I stared harder out the window.

"Well, well, well," said Beege, "and what happened to you, old man?" Old man, my aching head! I might have known he'd pick a time like that to take a big brotherly interest in me.

"Shut up," I hissed at him. Then in case he didn't get the hint, I gave him a little kick on the shin. It was hardly anything, though. He didn't have to hit me back so hard. Right on the knee, too. I thought I'd die.

"Listen, Andrew, what's the big idea? And I repeat, what happened to you? Mom, did you see Andrew?"

Well, I knew then that I was in for it, especially after Migsy turned around, looked at me, and gasped. "Hey, Andrew, you're all wet!"

Then Mom turned and looked at me and almost ran into a light post. She pulled over to the curb and stopped the car. "All right, young man, what did happen to you? Oh, this is too much! It's simply too much!" I could see Mom's neck get all tight and wiry like a bunch of piano strings.

"I'm sorry, Mom," I said. "These guys were having a water fight in the boys' room while I was in there getting ready to go. I slipped and fell. That's all."

"That's all! That's *all!* Andrew, couldn't you have left when you saw what was going on? And what do you mean, a water fight in the boys' room? What kind of school *is* that? I'm going to telephone the principal tomorrow. I'm going to—oh, I don't know what I'm going to do." Mom threw her head into her arms and leaned on the steering wheel. Then she said in a kind of muffled voice, "What time is it?"

"Eleven o'clock, Mom," Beege said.

"Well, we haven't time to stop off at the house. The ceremony starts at eleven-thirty, and Dad said he'd meet us in the lobby at fifteen after. Oh, Andrew, how could you do this to him?"

I didn't answer because, to be honest, I didn't know how I could. And I'll tell you something else. I was beginning to feel like this whole thing really was my crummy fault.

Mom sighed. "Well," she said, "I guess we'll just have to go on. You'll have to try to dry off as much as you can before we get there."

This was a very interesting piece of advice, but I knew Mom was upset enough, so I didn't comment on it. I did try to look helpful, though, and started to blow on myself, on my sleeves and down into my jacket. Beege snickered, naturally, and then shook his head like I was this hopeless case or something.

"Oh, go blow," I told him, but not out loud because I didn't want to start anything and rile Mom up some more. I just quit and stared out the window again. It was a pretty quiet ride to the Pentagon.

Dad met us on schedule. "What happened to you, son?" he asked me right away. I was still pretty wet. Dad didn't sound mad. I guess he just wanted to know.

"It's too long a story. We'll have to tell you about it later," Mom told him, at the same time trying to dust me off a little. I could see then that I'd managed to pick up something besides water, like a lot of dirt down my front when I'd tried to crawl out from under the cubicle. "Is there any place we can stop and fix him up so he'll look respectable?"

"We haven't time," Dad said. "We've got to get up there. Just straighten your tie, Andrew, and let's get going." Dad and Mom started on down the hall, and we followed after them.

Your dad never gets as shook up about the way you look as your mom does, and I knew that Dad probably had too much on his mind to worry about the mess I was in. But I figured that he had to care some. I tried to straighten my tie and shirt as we all marched down the hall, but I didn't think I was having much luck. I needed a mirror. When we passed this big glass case with a lot of printed instructions inside, I hung back to try and see myself in the glass. It didn't work, but right next to the glass case happened to be a door. And the door happened to say "Men."

The family parade was going on down the hall and didn't seem to notice that I'd dropped back. It looked like they had a way to go before there was a turnoff. I decided that I could duck into the room, take a quick look in the mirror, get myself into shape, and get back out again before they disappeared. So I went in. The situation in the mirror looked hopeless, but at least I tucked in my shirt and gave my tie a yank, and that made me feel better. Also I examined the lump that was developing on the top of my head and gave my hair a slick down over it. Then I hurled myself out of there.

I wasn't in there ten seconds, but when I got back

out into the hall, the family had disappeared. I suddenly realized that there were two other places that you could turn off before the end of the hall. I felt sunk, but I decided to take my chances on the end turnoff. I tore down the hall and ended up at what I guessed was the inside ring of the Pentagon the way Dad had explained it to us once. The only thing was, you could turn right or left around the ring, or go up some stairs straight ahead. I settled for the stairs and took them two at a time. There were no Kelloggs in sight there either. I took the stairs three at a time going back down.

It's funny how spooked you can get when you're in this big safe building. I mean, you're not even surrounded by wild beasts or enemy agents or stuff like that, but I felt like I was three years old and had gotten separated from my mom at the grocery store or something.

I couldn't figure out why nobody had missed me and come back for me. It was pretty unflattering. But there I was, yours truly, Andrew Kellogg, lost in the Pentagon. I wondered if Mrs. Rasmussen would have had the class give me a round of applause for that.

Well, I had to decide something. One plan was to stay put and hope somebody would come back looking for me. The second plan was to go find the others myself. It was the one I decided to follow. My motto has always been, What's the use of standing around when you can do something to really foul yourself up? I saw this open door near where I was standing, and a girl, a secretary I guess, was sitting at a desk there typing. She looked pretty busy. I was scared to go in, but I did. I stood in front of the desk, waiting for her to see me. She didn't, so I coughed.

Then she looked up at me, stopped her typing, and smiled.

"Hi," she said.

"Hi," I said.

She went back to her typing, but I guess she finally decided I wasn't going to blow away, so she smiled at me again.

"Can I help you, sonny?"

I hate being called sonny. It makes you feel like a little kid or something. But she was pretty with blonde hair piled all over her head, and she had a neat smile. I couldn't get as mad as I wanted to. I just tried to look like I was maybe sixteen and knew what I was doing. I put my hands in my pockets, looked around the room, and coughed again.

"Uh, nice office you have here," I said.

"Thank you," she said. "Is there someone you'd like to see? Colonel Bellows or Major Coughlin? May I tell them who's calling?"

"Uh, no thanks," I said. "I mean, I don't want to see those people. The person I—uh—want to see is General Turner." General Turner was the one who was going to present the medal to Dad.

"Oh, I see," she said, and her eyebrows went up. She was still smiling at me, though. "Well, this isn't General Turner's office. Do you know what room he's in?"

"No, I don't," I said. That's all I said, though. I wasn't going to mention getting lost from my family or anything like that. Heck, anyone could probably get lost in the Pentagon. You don't have to run around advertising *how* you got lost, for Pete's sake.

The secretary pulled a directory from her desk drawer. "Well here, we'll just look it up for you." It didn't take her a minute to find General Turner's room number and give me directions for getting there.

Now, I'm not personally criticizing the government or anything, but they really ought to provide seeing-eye dogs in the Pentagon even if you can see okay. It sounded pretty neat and simple when Dad explained to us about the halls called rings that go around the Pentagon, and about the halls that connect the rings, but when you're actually inside the place, Dad could have been explaining about the moon for all the good it did. What I'm trying to say is that I got my crummy self lost again.

I wandered down the hall trying to find the place the secretary told me to turn so I could go up some stairs. I never did find the stairs. I don't know what I did. All I know is that when I finally decided I'd better stop in another office and get some more directions, I was standing in the same office I'd just left, in front of the same secretary.

"Welcome back," she said. "I guess my directions weren't too good."

"Oh, they were swell. I mean, they were very nice directions. They weren't bad directions at all. I just couldn't—that is, I just didn't . . ." I decided to end my brilliant soliloquy.

"Well, it's my fault," she said, giving me a real nice smile. "I should have kept you here and telephoned General Turner's office. I did telephone after you left to let them know that a—uh—gentleman was on his way up. That is, in case they were expecting you . . ." I guess she was apologizing for poking into my business, but I felt pretty sunk anyway. She knew everything. I started to back away out into the hall.

"Hey, where are you going?" she asked.

"Uh, I'll try it again, I guess," I said.

"Not without me," she said and got up from her desk. "I think I'd better take you on up there. They sent someone to look for you as soon as they missed you, but whoever it was has probably given up by now. Anyway, I told them you'd probably be right there. We don't want to get you lost again."

She was neat, pretty and nice and all that. Walking along with her, I tried to feel like I was this big important person there on business or something. But all I felt like was a big hunk of junk being led back to his mommy and daddy. She was neat, though, and asked me a lot of questions about how long we'd been here and Dad's medal and all that. She didn't act like I was just a twelve-year-old kid. And she never called me sonny again the whole time. When we got to General Turner's office, she kind of squeezed my arm and said, "I hope you're not too late. Good luck!" She didn't even laugh when I stumbled over the rug going in.

The room I walked into was the reception room for the General's office, and it was filled with a lot of people. There was a family sitting there all dressed up and smiling, but they weren't Kelloggs. I wondered what they were doing there, but I didn't get to look at them much, because I'd barely walked in when an older looking lady from one of the secretary's desks got up and ran at me.

"Thank goodness you finally made it! You must be

Andrew Kellogg," she said, putting her arm around me. I dodged it a little, but I guess it could have been worse. She looked as if she was going to *kiss* me, for Pete's sake. She practically dragged me over to another door, but we had to stand back as a bunch of men with cameras came out. "Oh dear, I guess you're too late," she said, pushing me through.

And I was. Dad had already been presented with his medal, and they'd taken the pictures and everything. I felt sunk. Mom was looking proud, and she was smiling so hard at Dad it looked as if her face would split. When she saw me, though, she started to look as if she was hurting someplace. I saw her turn and start to say something to a tall, gray-haired man in an Air Force uniform standing next to her, but Dad interrupted. "General, this is Andrew," he said. "Andrew, this is General Turner."

"I'm happy to meet you, Andrew," General Turner said, squeezing my hand so hard I thought it would crack. I didn't mind, though. I like shaking hands like that. "And don't feel too bad about losing yourself in this place. It's easy to do. I'm just sorry we couldn't delay the ceremony, son. Unfortunately, we had to schedule another presentation just a few minutes from now. I'm sure you saw the family waiting outside my office. At any rate, you'll have pictures of all your family and one of your dad receiving his medal."

"Oh, that's okay, sir," I said. It wasn't really okay, though, missing the whole thing. If I'd been a little kid, I probably would have bawled. And furthermore, even though I wasn't getting it from Mom and Dad right then, I knew I'd be hearing plenty when we got home, especially from Mom and good old Beege. I felt terrible. I only wished I could think of something great and important to say, but I couldn't.

"Well, I know you're proud of your dad, Andrew. Maybe someday you'll earn a medal from the Air Force like this one."

All I had to say was something nice and humble like, "I hope so, sir," and then shut up. But I was so busy thinking about how I had to say some great thing and be the big deal, that instead I came out with, "Oh, I probably never will, sir, unless they give them in the Navy."

Now, I personally don't have anything against the Navy, but I'd never given one minute's thought to joining up. I guess I thought I was being funny. It didn't sound funny.

Dad's eyes opened up wide. I don't blame him, this being the first time he'd heard anything about it. I don't mean that Dad has ever expected us to be in the Air Force when we grow up or anything like that, but your dad likes it when you at least talk like you might want to do what he's doing, even if you end up never doing it. It's kind of respectful and shows you're proud of him, I guess. What I said was crummy.

"I didn't know you had a Navy man in the family, Bill," General Turner said. Then he laughed like I *had* said something funny, which was pretty neat of him. "Anyway, Andrew, whatever you end up doing either in the Navy, Army, Air Force, or as a civilian, if you do as good a job of it as your father has with the Air Force, and I'm sure you will, then your whole family will have something to be proud of."

All that made me feel like a bigger crumb than ever. And the thing was that I never said one word to Dad about his medal, like congratulations or anything. Not one rotten, lousy word.

While we were driving home, and the whole time we were having lunch at the Hot Shoppe, which Mom allowed us to do since this was a special occasion, all Migsy did was talk about what had happened when Dad got his medal. There was all that stuff about the citation being read by General Turner, and then even Mom got something read about her too, saying what a help she'd been to Dad.

I'm not saying I didn't care about all this, but I thought being lost in the Pentagon was pretty interesting, too. I mean, it's not exactly what you'd call a small place with twenty-five thousand people working there. I could have disappeared forever, if anyone would care to know. But every time I opened my mouth with some interesting piece of information about myself, I got drowned out by Migsy and her news. Or else I got told to shut up by Beege. I guess I just should have been grateful not to get my ears pinned back for getting lost in the first place.

After I changed my clothes and got back to school, I had the pleasure of being reminded about Arthur and Melvin again, which I needed like a million extra holes in the head. I learned one thing, though. I'll never make the mistake of asking to go to the boys' room during class again. I decided that from then on, even if I was half dead from having to go, I'd just stay at my desk and suffer until the bell rang.

When I got home from school, I went up to my room and shut the door. Grover scratched on the door right away, so I let *him* in. Then I just goofed around a while. I took out my stamps, put them back in the desk drawer, and took out my knife instead. I started carving some more in the top of my desk. This carving is pretty private. I keep it hidden under a large piece of blotting paper. It's this shield I'm making with my crest on it. I don't mean I really have a crest. I'm just making one up. It's going to be a tiger rampant on a field of doves. Right now the tiger looks like a beagle, though. I might keep it that way. I like dogs better than anything.

I didn't carve for long, because pretty soon I heard something banging outside and moved to my window seat to see what was going on. It was just Beege throwing baskets and hitting the garage door with the ball. Then I saw something else outside that made me shove up my window.

"Hey, Migsy, what're you doing?" I shouted.

"Feeding my baby," said Migsy.

"Mealworms?" I screamed back. I recognized the big jar I'd stored the worms in. It had a red label that I couldn't miss even from way up at my window. The thing is that Migsy was putting the mealworms inside her doll carriage, which she was pushing around the yard.

"What kind of baby do you *have* in that carriage?"

"A baby," said Migsy, feeding another worm to something under the hood.

I decided I'd go look into this, so I took Grover and went down to the backyard over to Migsy's doll carriage. It was old Glorious, all right, sitting on a doll pillow and wrapped around with this pink lace cover that used to be on Migsy's bed when she was a baby. It was pretty funny. I have to admit it. But I wondered if it was healthy for Glorious. Also, he was eating up a whole pile of his winter supplies.

"Look, Migs," I said, "this is a pretty cute baby and all that, but don't you ever give it a bath?"

"He's just had a bath," Migsy informed me, wasting another mealworm on that big hog in the doll carriage.

"He looks dirty to me, especially behind the ears."

"Do you really think so?" Migsy asked.

"Filthy," I said. "You'd better put him back in the bathtub. That's his *pool*, Migs."

"Okay."

I was surprised that she gave in so easily, but she wheeled her carriage right around and started back toward the pool. It was that dumb frog that didn't want to go back to his home, though, and when Migsy picked him up, he jumped out of her hands.

"Allow me," I said and went after him. Unfortunately, so did Grover.

I could have caught Glorious without any trouble, but it isn't too easy to catch a frog when your dog is barking at it and jumping all over you at the same time. Glorious went under a bush and back out again when Grover got to him, and the next thing he did was head over to the driveway where Beege was shooting baskets.

Then this big, fat, healthy frog jumped right over to Beege's feet and suddenly got very tired. Grover stopped barking and just stood looking up at Beege and wagging his rotten tail. The traitor. So all Beege had to do was lean over and pick Glorious up, stroll over to the pool, and set him down on his lily pad, from which Glorious jumped immediately into the water. Migsy rewarded Beege with a big smile, naturally. No matter what he does, he always comes up the big deal.

"See here, John Paul Jones," he said to me, "the next time you need help launching the U.S. Navy, just call on the experts."

To tell the truth, I had temporarily forgotten about that beautiful remark. I might have known Beege wouldn't. He'd remember it until he died.

"Oh, that's brilliant," I said. "I didn't know you could be so brilliant."

"What's wrong? Did I step on the royal naval toe?" Beege gave me a short bow from the waist.

"You just shut up about it!"

"Watch your language, young man," Beege said. He started to wear this know-it-all grin. "What's wrong? Have you given up the idea of going to sea already? Tsk. Tsk."

"Maybe I have and maybe I haven't. It's none of your business, and you just shut up about it!"

"Well, it's my business when my younger brother embarrasses me to death and goes around ruining the day for everyone."

"I did not!"

"Look, Andrew," said Beege, pretending to give me a bored yawn, "this whole thing is plainly over your head. But let me just give you a brotherly tip. Shape up! Maybe if you try real hard, you might be able to do *some-*

thing without lousing it up. Who knows, you might even do something worthwhile someday." He went strolling back to the basketball net without looking at me.

"Yeah," I said to his back, "something worthwhile like catching a crummy frog. Big deal!" Beege picked up his basketball and started shooting baskets again. He never answered me.

Migsy knew better than to get in the conversation, so she pulled a real doll from somewhere in her carriage, fixed it up on the pink lace cover, and went wheeling all prim and motherly out the gate.

I took Grover and went slamming back into the house. I was going to go slamming on down the driveway, but I suddenly remembered a telephone call I was supposed to make. Mr. Cummings, who is this dealer for the *Washington Post*, told me the week before that he might have a paper route that I could have. It wasn't in our neighborhood, but he didn't tell me exactly where it was. Anyway, he told me to call him later when he'd know something more definite.

"Well, Andrew," he said when I got him on the telephone, "I think you're in luck. The route is yours if you want it."

"Where is it, sir?" I asked.

"That might present a problem," he said. "The route is about a mile from your home. Do you think you could manage that? I'd want you to think about this pretty carefully before you took it."

My heart sank a little. I'd have to bike over there dragging my wagon behind me, and it's pretty hilly going around where we live. I wasn't sure if my bike would make it. Then it came to me that with one month's salary I could get a new bike and I'd be in.

"Oh, a mile isn't too bad, Mr. Cummings," I told him. "I could do it."

Mom just happened to be in the kitchen then, which is where our telephone is.

"A mile? A mile to what? You could do *what*, Andrew? What are you getting yourself into?" she said.

"Just a moment, Mr. Cummings, my mom wants to tell me something."

"Yes, I certainly do," she said. "And who is Mr. Cummings?"

"Mom," I said, trying to be very patient and not get her all riled up, "I told you before about Mr. Cummings. He's the dealer from the *Washington Post*. He has this paper route for me. It's a mile from here, but I can do it, Mom. Honest!"

"A paper route a mile from here!" She practically screamed it. "I wouldn't let you take one half a mile from here, and I'm sure your father wouldn't either. Dear, you're only twelve and you've never had a paper route before. And, well, you know . . ."

"No, I don't know," I said. "And, Mom, I've got to learn some time."

"Yes, of course, you do. But it doesn't have to be a mile from home and at five o'clock in the morning. I imagine that's the time you'd have to start out for a morning route. Just tell your Mr. Cummings absolutely no. I admire your wanting to do this, dear, but it's out of the question. Perhaps if you weren't—well, never mind. You just ask him to please keep your name on file for the neighborhood route."

I knew what Mom was going to say about "Perhaps if you weren't." It was perhaps if I weren't *Andrew*. Being twelve had nothing to do with it.

I asked Mr. Cummings to call me when a route came up near us, but I knew it wouldn't do any good. All three newspapers had told me the routes in our neighborhood were sewed up tight by guys who had had them at least a couple of years, and it didn't look like they'd ever quit unless they died or something.

Well, I got to feeling sorrier for myself than ever. Here was Mom practically out and out telling me I couldn't handle a paper route, on top of Beege just telling me that I was a big crumb doomed to go around messing up my whole crummy life, on top of getting my crummy self lost at the Pentagon.

I sat around my room for about as long as I could stand it, which happened to be near suppertime, and then marched noisily out of the house. I was hoping someone would ask me where I thought I was going at that hour so we could maybe have a fight. But nobody did, so all I did was end up going for a lousy walk by myself.

Seven

IT WAS getting pretty dark, dark enough so the streetlights were coming on when I went past Sally Ardery's house.

"Hi, Andrew!"

I was going at such a fast clip that I was practically at the next house before I realized that anyone had said anything. I turned around and there was Sally.

She was sitting on her front steps looking kind of sad and lonely. Her school books were on the step beside her as if she'd been doing her homework out there. I thought it was a strange place to be doing your homework, especially since it was getting dark and cold.

Sally had turned out to be in the seventh grade, too. I don't have her in my homeroom, so she's not in any of my regular classes, but we're in French together. French is the subject you get to elect if you don't take woodshop and stuff like that. French is a good idea in case Dad ever gets stationed in Europe and I need to get around in Paris. What I mean is, Mom and Dad told me I had to take French, and so I'm taking it because I didn't want to start another family crisis. Anyway, Sally's in that class.

She's pretty popular. At lunchtime, if I see her in the cafeteria, she's always surrounded by kids. You can usually hear someone saying, "Hey, there's Sally!" or "Let's not sit here. Let's go sit with Sally!" Then they rush up to her table and get turned away because someone else rushed there first. She's really one of the big deals in the seventh grade.

That's why I got this queer feeling seeing her sitting all alone in front of her house. Since that one time she talked to me when I first walked by her house, we'd never talked together. I tried to think of something clever to say.

"Hi!" That was what I said.

Sally drew her knees up to her chin and smiled at me. "It's getting pretty cold, isn't it?"

"Yeah," I said. Then I got brilliant. "I mean, *oui, oui.*" *Oui, oui* is French for *yeah.*

Sally laughed. "Do you like French?" she asked me.

"Sometimes," I said. I do like it sometimes. Like right then, for instance.

"Me too," Sally said. "I mean, *moi aussi.*"

I laughed too, but I couldn't think of anything more to say in French. I couldn't even think of anything more to say in English.

"Look, Andrew," Sally said as I was standing around trying to think up something brilliant or even semi-brilliant to say. "It's nice of you to stay here with me, but you don't have to, really. I'll be all right."

That really knocked me over. All I'd thought about was that *she* was being neat talking to *me*. I didn't know *I* was doing anything so great.

"Oh—uh—I don't have anyplace to go," I said. "What I mean is, are you—waiting for someone?" I didn't want to be nosy, but I thought I ought to ask.

"Yes," Sally said.

"Uh, couldn't you wait in your house? I mean, it would be warmer and all that."

"That's just the problem. I can't get in the house. I lost my key, and I'm waiting for Father to come home and let me in."

That was pretty disappointing. I mean, I was beginning to hope there'd be a more exciting explanation, maybe even dangerous. Losing your door key is sort of tame. Still, Sally looked really sad sitting out there alone, and I decided not to leave her even if I was late for dinner and got my ears pinned back.

"Is he going to be home soon?" I asked.

"Usually he's home by now," Sally said. "If he isn't, it means he's working late. He probably telephoned, but I was over at Lynda Brecker's house doing homework with her. He always telephones so I don't need to have dinner ready so early."

"Doesn't your mom get dinner?" I asked. Then I looked at the dark house. "Oh, I guess she isn't home either."

"No—no, she isn't." Sally's voice sounded so funny that I looked at her to see what was wrong, but she had her face turned away.

"I guess she works too," I said, sounding pretty lame.

Sally didn't answer me. I decided then that I'd just better keep my big mouth shut about her mother. "Look," I said, "is there any way I can get into the house? Is there a window open somewhere?"

"Yes, there is, but it's on the second floor. The spare bedroom window is unlocked, and you can push it open. There's no screen on it because I have a bird feeder there. But it's too high. No one could get up there to open it." She pointed to a window just about over our heads. There was a tree growing next to it.

"Doesn't that tree go near the window?" I asked.

"Yes. There's a big branch that grows right up to it. But don't get any crazy ideas."

Well, I'm no Robin Hood, but on the other hand I've never had any damsel in distress to rescue either or be the big deal around. It changes the picture of things.

"It's nothing. I could do it."

"Please don't, Andrew!"

But I was already on my way over.

I can't make out like it was such a big deal climbing that tree. I mean, it wasn't like climbing a slippery drainpipe or anything like that. But it was pretty spooky when I had to reach out from the last branch and grab at the windowsill to pull myself over. When I looked down to the ground and saw all that thin air between me and it, I didn't care *who* was in distress—I was going back down the safe way. I didn't, though. I tell you, you have to be careful when you get mixed up with girls. You never know what you're going to end up doing. Your brain goes soft, I guess. I said a small prayer and reached out for the window. I made it and heard Sally give a gasp. It's worth it, trying to be the big deal around a girl.

I pushed the window up and then climbed in around the bird feeder. I knocked into the feeder, though, and spilled a bunch of birdseed down on Sally's head. You might know I'd end up doing something beautiful like that. But I was too happy to be on a solid floor again to worry about it. I found the light switch and in about half a minute had lights on all the way down to the first floor. I let Sally in.

The first thing she said was, "Andrew, you're crazy. You shouldn't have done that. You could have killed yourself. You're really crazy." That was what she said, but I knew she didn't mean it, the part about being crazy. And I knew she was glad to be in her house and not sitting out there in the dark all alone. Right after that, though, she said something funny. "You know, it's nice to come into a house when all the lights are on. Thank you for turning on the lights, Andrew."

I didn't know what to say to that. I guess I'd never thought about it before, coming into a house where the lights are on. It was a funny thing for a kid to say, even a girl. Then Sally started *doing* something funny. She began to shake her head and dust her hair off with her hand.

"What's wrong?" I asked.

"I don't know. Just about the time you were climbing into the house, something fell on my head through the tree. I thought it was just a little dirt, but it's—it's *birdseed!*"

"Yeah," I said. "I guess I knocked the bird feeder climbing in the window. Boy, how clumsy can you get! I'll bet Robin Hood never spilled birdseed all over Maid Marian when he was climbing around rescuing *her.*"

Sally laughed. "Well, Robin Hood never had to climb around Maid Marian's bird feeder either!"

"Yeah," I said. I was feeling pretty good. I have to admit it. "Well, will you be okay now?"

"Sure. Thanks a lot, but wouldn't you like to have a Coke before you go? You can have it in the kitchen while I'm starting dinner for Father."

I knew I shouldn't stay. It was really getting late.

"Yeah," I said, and followed her into the kitchen.

Then I kind of lounged around at the table the way I'd seen Beege do it, drinking my Coke and watching Sally getting stuff for their dinner. I was feeling like the big deal. I have to admit it.

Suddenly Sally cried out, "Oh no!"

"What's wrong?" I asked.

"Oh, it's nothing much, I guess. I'm sorry. It's just that I was going to go to the store for some sugar this afternoon. We're completely out, and I was going to bake Mother's favorite cake for her after school tomorrow. It's her birthday."

"Could you get it tomorrow?" I asked.

"No. I have to stay late after school for a class meeting, and by the time I get out it'll be too late to go to the store and bake a cake besides. I guess I'll just have to forget about it."

"No, you won't," I said. "Look, I can ride down on my bike and get the sugar for you after school and bring it over. I'll probably have it here before you get home."

"Would you really?" Sally asked.

"Yeah," I said. I didn't go into details about what a dangerous expedition it would be on my ancient bike. Anyway, I'd even have gone so far as to walk. Then suddenly something struck me. "I thought your mom wasn't home."

Sally started shuffling stuff around on the counter. "She's coming home for the weekend," she said. Her voice was quiet and level.

"Has she gone on a trip? That's neat."

"No. She's sick. She's at a sanitarium, and she comes home on weekends."

"Oh, that's good. I mean, that she's coming home and all that." I ended up sounding lame-brained and jerky. I wished I'd kept my big mouth shut. I sure didn't want Sally thinking I was this big nosy person. I decided it was time I went home.

I couldn't help wondering, though, when I was on my way home what was wrong with Mrs. Ardery, and how long she'd been sick with whatever it was she was sick with. I remembered the first time I'd ever seen Sally when she was out trimming the hedge in her yard. With her mom sick in a sanitarium and her dad working late a lot, I guessed that Sally probably did a lot of stuff like that, besides cooking and everything else. It was funny to think of a kid my age, even if she was a girl, doing all that stuff.

I thought about Sally again when I walked into our house, about what she'd said about walking into a house with the lights on. Even when you know you're going to get your ears pinned back for being late for dinner, it's nice to walk into your house and have someone home, and the table set, and the smell of something good coming from the kitchen, and everything all warm and bright. Mom still wasn't the way she used to be, getting upset so easily and stuff like that, but at least she was Mom and she was *there*, if you know what I mean.

Anyway, by the time I'd arrived home, I'd cooled off and wasn't mad anymore, or feeling sorry for myself. After all, what did I have to be so sorry about!

As soon as I got back from school the next day, I hopped on my bike and started out for the store. On my way down the driveway, Migsy stopped me.

"Andrew, when are we going to move Glorious into the house? It's cold and he's going to freeze to death."

"Look, Migsy," I said, "this weekend. I promise." I meant it too. But I wasn't going to stop right then and worry about a crummy frog when I had this big deal errand to run for Sally. I promised Migsy that if I had time I'd stop at the pet store and pick up some more mealworms. This satisfied her.

All the way to the store I kept hoping one of the kids from school would see me and ask me where I was going. Then I could tell them that I was just doing this little favor for Sally Ardery, and how she was my neighbor, and what good friends we were, and anything else that came to my mind. What I hoped most, though, was that when I delivered the sugar to Sally, she'd invite me in again for a Coke.

I went to the grocery store before I went to the pet shop in case I didn't have time for both. And I decided to buy a ten-pound bag of sugar so it would look like a bigger deal when I delivered it to Sally. I planned to tell her it was a present from me, and I wasn't going to let her pay for it. Following this beautiful thinking, I decided to tell the grocery checker not to put the sugar in a sack. My idea was that anyone who saw me would be curious about what the sugar was for so I could still tell them all the stuff about Sally and me.

I had enough time and just about enough money after that to get to the pet store and pick up some mealworms for Glorious. After buying the worms, I had a little money left over, which I should have saved because I knew it was going to take me about ten years to save up for my bike if a paper route didn't come through. But I happened to see this neat green stuff growing in a fish tank that I knew Migsy would blow her brains over for Glorious, making his gloomy new home in the basement tropical and cheerful and all that. I told the pet shop guy I'd take some, so he grabbed a handful of it, put it in a small box with a handle on it, ladled in some water, and closed the top. There was just enough room in my bike basket for the worms, the box, and the sugar.

Up until then I hadn't seen anyone I knew. This was pretty disappointing, but life is full of sad stuff like that. You have to face it, I told myself, and wavered off on my bicycle.

Then I finally saw someone I knew, a couple of people coming out of the Thirty-one Flavors ice-cream place, drooling and slobbering over triple-decker ice-cream cones. These were not the people I had in mind when I said I wanted to meet someone I knew. They were Arthur Kogel and Melvin Funkhauser.

I was headed right toward them, and there wasn't any way I could turn and go in the opposite direction without getting myself draped over a couple of cars. So I just put my head down and raced past them as fast as I could go. On my bike that happens to be about one mile per hour. Needless to say, they saw me.

"Hey, there goes Paul Revere! What'd you do with your horse, Paul? Hey, Cornflakes, you lost your horse," Melvin yelled after me.

Arthur delivered a catcall.

"Let's go after him," Melvin hollered.

"Aw, let's finish these cones first," screamed Arthur. "We can finish them and *still* catch up with him!" This was followed by a lot of hoots and more catcalls.

I got about half a block away and then like a big jerk turned my head to see if they were following. They weren't, but my bike quivered in the wrong direction and before I knew what was happening, I'd run right up on the curb and into a fire hydrant. My bike didn't go all the way over, but all those ten pounds of sugar did. Also the mealworms and the tropical green stuff. Splat! The sugar bag busted wide open, and the water and the green stuff landed right on top of the sugar that spilled out. The worms were right in the middle of it all.

"Hey, Cornflakes has had an accident!"

"Poor fellow! Let's go help him out!" I could hear Arthur and Melvin yelling.

I knew how much help I'd be getting from *those* guys. There was no time to try to rescue any of the sugar, which was in pretty bad shape anyway, but I grabbed for the plastic bags of worms, stuffed them in my back pocket, and took off. It just about knocked me out to leave all that sugar for those crumbs to laugh over. Not to mention all my nice green tropical stuff.

I didn't know what to do then. Even more than presenting Sally with practically a whole grocery store full of sugar, the thing I wanted to do most was be there with it when she got home. That left me one choice, borrow the sugar from Mom.

Mom wasn't around when I got home, though. Neither was Migsy, and I forgot all about the worms in my pocket. The door to Mom and Dad's room was closed, so I figured Mom might be taking a nap. I didn't want to wake her, so I thought I'd just go ahead and help myself to the sugar. Mom being Mom, that's what she'd want me to do if Sally needed it.

The only problem was that I couldn't find a spare bag of sugar around, so I ended up taking a brown grocery sack and emptying all the sugar from the sugar bowl into it, plus all the sugar from the can on top of the counter. I figured there was extra sugar stored away someplace and it wouldn't matter if I took all that I could find.

I ran down to Sally's house and rang the doorbell. Nobody answered so I rang again. Then I knocked and then rang again. I was just congratulating myself that I'd beaten Sally home and was getting ready to sit down on the steps and wait for her, when the door opened and there was this lady standing there. I was pretty surprised, because Sally hadn't said anything about having a house-keeper.

"Well, hello there," the lady said. "I thought you might be Sally coming home."

"Yeah. I mean, I'm not," I said.

The lady smiled. "Is there anything I can help you with?"

"I brought this for Sally," I said, and handed her the grocery sack. "It's—uh—sugar."

The lady took it. "Well, isn't that kind of you. I'll certainly tell Sally when she gets home."

"Uh, she's out of it," I said. I thought I'd better say it so the lady wouldn't think I was some kind of idiot delivering grocery sacks full of sugar around the neighborhood.

"I know," the lady said, and she laughed. "I just found it out. My husband was able to bring me home early this afternoon, and now he's gone out to pick up some groceries for our dinner. But I must confess that sugar was *not* on the list. Thank you so much. By the way, you haven't told me your name."

"Andrew."

"Well, Andrew, thank you again. I'm Mrs. Ardery. Would you like to come in and wait for Sally?"

"Yeah," I said. "I mean, I'd like to, but I have this place to go to. Uh, thanks a lot." I nearly broke my neck backing off the steps.

I was really knocked over. Here I'd thought I was

talking to a housekeeper and it turned out to be Mrs. Ardery. I should have guessed with the eyes she had, big green ones like Sally's. And she had the same neat smile. But I'd thought Mrs. Ardery was sick. She didn't look sick to me. She didn't even *act* sick. But suddenly I remembered the thing that Arthur Kogel had said to me right after we'd arrived. The thing about Sally's mother being crazy. And Sally had said she was in a sanitarium, so that meant she *had* to be sick. I put it all together and realized that Mrs. Ardery must have been sick with something in the brain department. Well, so what! She was no different from anyone else's mom. Nicer than most I'd met. But you'd have to expect that a guy like Arthur would use a word like crazy.

I'd like to have stayed around and waited for Sally, but I have to be honest, I was pretty shook up finding out it was Mrs. Ardery I was talking to. Besides, I'd already said I had a place to go, so I figured I was stuck with it. The truth is that I didn't really have anyplace to go at all. You just say stuff like that when you can't think of anything else. However, I happen to be a person who thinks that when you say you're going someplace, you ought to go there even if you have to think up a place to go.

Anyway, that's how I ended up going back to the Chinese mansion even though I'd told myself several thousand times that it would be much healthier for yours truly, Andrew S. Kellogg, if I never saw it again.

Eight

I NEVER had any plans at all when I got to the mansion. I swear it. All I was going to do was just lurk outside the grounds a while, maybe spot the little Chinese lady, and then go home. But I should have known that I'd start having my usual one-man conversation with myself. By the time I'd ended it, I had one foot up on the cement wall, another on the first iron rung, and was hoisting myself over the fence.

Once I was inside, I tried to persuade myself to climb back out again, but it didn't work. I'd lurked around just long enough to convince myself that the Chinese mansion had deep, maybe even sinister, secrets, and I, Andrew, Super Spy from the West, was going to find them out or bust. I'd be famous. The F.B.I. would give me a medal. Mom would change her mind about the paper route. And I'd show Beege a thing or two. He'd find out what a big deal his kid brother really was.

My heart was pounding so hard I could barely breathe, but by then, nothing was going to stop me. I ducked down behind the bushes that ran the width of the fence and waited to see if anyone was coming down the path on the other side of them, the one where I'd first seen the Chinese lady. A couple of squirrels nearly sent me back over the fence, but I stuck it out and finally decided I was the only human-type being around. Then I raced across the path and hid among some more bushes.

I must have done this same thing about four more times. The garden was really wild, more like a forest than anything else. I could barely see the house through the bushes and trees as I headed for it. But I finally came to a deep ravine and there it was, right on the other side, the house of Robert E. Lee's Chinese descendants!

It looked it, the exact kind of house I'd expected Robert E. Lee would have. It was built of red brick and was bigger than practically four of our house put together. And even though I was coming at it from the side, I could see that there were these great pillars along the front. But I still had trouble believing it. The only Robert E. Lee's house I'd ever heard about was in another part of town. What was this one doing here? Why wasn't it ever mentioned in the guidebooks? Why was this great historical building hidden from the whole world?

I stumbled down the ravine with my brain revolving at a hundred twenty RPM. Unfortunately, in my stupor, I waded right into a stream at the bottom of it, which nearly ended the expedition. Besides being uncomfortable, it's downright dangerous to go spying around in a pair of soggy sneakers. You make this loud, sucking sound with every step. But I'd gone too far to turn back, so I raced across the final path to the house and shoved my way through the bushes around it.

It wasn't until then, when I stood up beside the house, that I discovered the ground floor windows were way over my head. There was no way to see inside. What would I do next? Nothing, I had to admit finally. I was no human-type fly that could go around scaling drainpipes. "Some spy," I said to myself in disgust, and decided I might as well go home.

Then suddenly, right where I was standing, a light went on at my feet. I leaped to one side, ready to make a run for it, but my wet sneakers didn't feel like leaping with me, and I fell over into the bushes with a crunching thud. Naturally, I thought I'd stepped on this ancient Oriental booby trap, and I lay there with my eyes closed, preparing to die.

When nothing happened, however, and I realized that my miserable life had been spared, I opened my eyes cautiously and looked back toward the light. All it was, was that somebody had turned on a crummy light in a basement room with a window right about where I'd been standing. I have to admit it was pretty disappointing, but I decided I might as well crawl over and have a look.

Now, usually when you look in a basement, you see stuff like water heaters, busted picture frames, lawn mowers, old shoes, and stuff like that. Maybe that's why what I did see made my brain go into orbit. I mean even more than usual.

What I saw through that basement window was no

ordinary basement, but a big room all white and clean and filled on one side with gym equipment. The other side was empty. There was no one in the room, but as I lay on my stomach staring in, the person who must have turned on the light came back. It was a man, and with him was a kid about my age. And they were both Chinese!

They were wearing white suits and carrying fencing foils and masks, which they put on after they'd come into the room. After only a few minutes, I could tell that what I was watching was a fencing lesson. The older guy was teaching the kid to fence. It was all I needed for my beautiful mind to go to work.

What kind of kid would be going in for this kind of stuff, and what kind of family would be seeing that he did unless he was in training for something? That was a pretty fancy gymnasium down there. Wow! But training for what? The Olympics? To be a leader of some kind, maybe? Leader of what?

Leader of *what*, Andrew old boy? I repeated. Well, buddy, if you've heard it once, you've heard it ten thousand times, I said, that the South has never stopped fighting the Civil War. So here is one of Robert E. Lee's Chinese descendants having all this military-type training.

The conclusion of this conversation is very hard to believe, but I swear it's what I ended up with—that this little Chinese guy was being trained to carry on the Civil War in the footsteps of his great-great-grandfather, Robert E. Lee!

Well, after all, facts were facts, and had I ever in my whole life had such neat facts as I had then, starting with the bronze plate and the words "Robert E. Lee" and the Chinese writing? And all taking place right in the heart of Robert E. Lee country? Even a guy with no imagination at all would have had trouble disputing all this.

I guess I was so carried away with my discovery, and what a big deal I was for having made it, that I never heard the footsteps coming down the path until they were practically on top of me, and it was too late to make a dash for it. All I could do was pray that the footsteps kept right on going. They didn't, and after only a few seconds, I got the feeling that someone was watching me.

Cautiously I parted the leaves of a bush and looked out with one eye. And there was the little old Chinese lady, Robert E. Lee's actual descendant, looking straight back into it! There was nothing left to do but stand up and reveal all of me.

I was sure that the lady would scream or faint· or something, but she didn't. She just kept standing there staring at me. I finally decided that she was waiting for some kind of explanation about what I was doing behind her azalea bushes, but I don't know enough Chinese to put in one ear. Except for this one thing a friend of Dad's taught me when I was a little guy. That's "How are you?"

"*How boohow?*" I said, plowing out through the bushes and onto the path.

The lady looked surprised for a moment and then said very calmly, "I'm very well, thank you. And how are you?" What I mean is, she said it in plain English.

From that point on my mind must have blanked out, because instead of giving this lady some explanation about what I was doing trespassing in her garden, I raised my right fist in the air and shouted, "The South will rise again! I mean, the South will rise again, *ma'am!*"

Then I turned and charged over to the ravine with my wet sneakers squishing every step of the way, stumbled over a low bush at the head of it, and fell crashing to the bottom. When I found that I was still alive, I staggered to my feet and, somehow, made my way home.

I wanted so badly to tell someone about my adventure that it almost hurt. A secret is a pretty miserable thing when you're the only one in the whole world who knows it. But there was only my family, and I knew I'd have to be half-cracked to tell them. It was only after I was famous that I'd ever let them know anything. Anyway, something happened right after I got home that put the whole crazy thing out of my head.

I was sitting upstairs in my room just before dinner, pulling on some dry socks, when I heard all this banging around in our kitchen. The banging wasn't real bad, just a couple of lids being slammed down and some drawers being slammed in. Still, I couldn't help wondering what was going on, so I wandered down to the kitchen.

Dad was there with Mom and Migsy. They were all storming through cupboards and jars and just about everything in sight. Mom looked a little hysterical, but it was the way she'd been looking so much lately that I was almost used to it.

"What's wrong?" I asked, helping myself to a piece of celery on the counter.

"Andrew," Mom said, "you didn't—oh no, no, you wouldn't have. What am I thinking of!"

"Wouldn't have what?"

"Your mother was all set to bake some cookies after dinner tonight, and she has somehow mysteriously run out of sugar since this morning—or some time." Dad sounded a little doubtful about the whole thing.

"Bill, it *was* this morning! Are you doubting that . . ."

"No, no, of course not, Sam."

"Mommy's right, Dad," Migsy said. "I know we had sugar in the sugar bowl because I used some on my cereal."

"There, you see!" Mom said.

"I'm sorry," Dad said, "but do you really have to bake these cookies, Sam? With all the other things you've got to do before—"

"I'm not going to depart from this house without leaving something for the children. I'm *going* to bake them cookies or a cake or—or something. Oh, Bill, I can't leave!" Mom threw herself into a kitchen chair and hid her face in her hands.

"Where's Mommy going, Daddy?" Migsy asked.

Dad looked at both Migsy and me and shook his head as if we weren't to say any more about it. "Look, Sam, it's all been decided, so no more of that. Now about that sugar—I'll run down to the store and get some as soon as we've finished dinner."

"But I don't see why you have to when I've got plenty here. I know I have!"

You're probably wondering why I was standing around watching all this going on without saying anything. I'll tell you why. If you think the roof is going to fall on your head when you open your big mouth, you think over a few things before you open it. I have to be honest. I wasn't sure whether I ought to admit anything or not. But when I saw that Mom was getting hysterical again, I broke down.

"I know where it is," I said quietly.

"You what?" Mom and Dad said it at the same time.

"Well, I borrowed it," I said.

"Andrew, would you please explain that?" Dad asked.

"Look, someone needed it so I lent it to them. I mean, I *gave* it to them!" I guess I was sounding pretty defensive. You know how it is when you've got your back up against a wall and they're ready to execute you.

"Andrew, you don't have to use that tone of voice. Your mother and I simply want to know what was so necessary about—"

"It was for Sally Ardery. The Arderys are the ones who live in that yellow house around the block from us. Her mom is sick, and Sally wanted to bake a cake for her. They were all out of sugar so I took some of ours."

"Took some! I should say you did. Couldn't you have asked your mother first if she had any to spare before taking the whole supply?"

"Mom was sleeping and I didn't want to wake her. Besides, I knew she'd say yes. She's always lending stuff to people, Dad. At least she used to. I mean—"

"Of course, dear," Mom said quickly. "You're right about lending or even giving friends something when they need it. Oh dear, I don't know why I'm getting so upset about anything so idiotic as a couple of pounds of sugar. I don't know what's wrong with me. I don't know anything anymore!" Mom was looking at the wall, but I could see tears rolling down her face. I couldn't stand it, watching her.

"Well," she said at last with a big sniffle, "we can't

sit around here forever. I'd better get dinner on the table." She went over to the sink, and with the tears still rolling down her face, started pulling plates from the cupboard.

"Don't just stand there, Andrew," Dad said. He sounded mad, but maybe it was only because he was all mixed-up inside the way I was. "Go get your brother and tell him dinner's ready."

I went and got Beege.

Maybe Mom would have been okay the rest of the evening. I don't know. But then I had to go and do it again. I'd forgotten all about those crummy worms in my pocket until I sat down at the table and heard this crunchy sound when my bottom struck the plastic bags. "Oh help!" I yelled, and then I pulled the bags out of my pocket.

Mealworms have strong constitutions. Even with me landing on them, a lot of them were in pretty good shape and wriggling around. The plastic bags were okay too, except that they were kind of sticky from sitting on wet sugar. I thought it was all pretty interesting, but nobody else thought so.

"Oh, Andrew, not at the dinner table!" Mom said. Then she busted out crying again.

"Andrew!" Dad shouted. "Haven't you done enough today? You take that stuff up to your room right now!"

"Oh, Bill, don't," Mom said, sobbing out loud. "Don't shout at him. I'm sorry!" She pushed herself away from the table and started running up the stairs. "I'm sorry! I'm sorry!" We could hear her saying it all the way to her room. Dad ran up after her.

Migsy and Beege and I stayed at the table pretending to eat. Everything was quiet for a while. Then Migsy started to cry.

"Boy, Andrew," Beege said, "I thought I told you to shape up. What's the big idea?"

"Lay off!" I said. "It's not *my* fault."

"Well, whose is it? You've been ruining Mom's life ever since we got here, lousing up the day at the Pentagon and everything else. What's the big idea of running around with a bunch of worms in your pocket? You think you're back in kindergarten or something?"

"You shut up! I can carry worms around if I feel like it. And I have not been ruining Mom's life. I have not! You just shut up!"

"Will you all please keep your voices down," Dad said, appearing back in the dining room. He sat down at the table. "Beege, I want you to leave your brother alone about this. We're all upset, and there's nothing to be gained by hurling a lot of accusations. That goes for me, too, Andrew. I'm sorry."

Dad started to take a bite of something and then suddenly put his fork down. "Look, kids," he said, "I've been trying to find a time to tell you this, and I guess this is as good as any. Your mother has been wanting to do it herself, but she just hasn't been able to. I was going to tell you tomorrow when we'd all be less tired, but the fact is that Mom is going to have to go away for a while for a rest."

Migsy pushed herself away from the table, ran over to Dad, and threw her arms around his neck. She was crying all over the place. "Mommy's going away! I knew she was going away! She's never coming back!"

Dad gave her a big hug and pulled her down on his

lap. Then he took a handkerchief from his pocket and wiped her nose. "Of course she's coming back. Piglet, you're going to have to be a big girl about this or you're not going to help Mommy one bit." He gave Migsy another hug.

"Where's Mom going, Dad?" Beege asked.

"I was coming to that. I guess it's no secret to you kids that your mother hasn't been herself since we got here. Since we left California, in fact. That bout with pneumonia took a lot out of her. Then she had to face leaving Micky in California, which was harder than you can imagine, and finally there were all the problems of getting settled here. Well, about two weeks ago, her doctors recommended that she get away somewhere for a complete rest."

"You mean somewhere like—like a sanitarium?" I asked.

"No, Andrew. Mom doesn't have to go to any hospital. Fortunately, as you all know, your Aunt Ann was a nurse and lives alone now in that big house in New York. We've written her and she wants Mom to come and stay with her. The doctors agree that it would be just the thing to help Mom get well."

I had thought about the sanitarium because of Mrs. Ardery. I was glad Dad didn't ask me any questions about it. I didn't want to talk about Mrs. Ardery. Not right then, anyway.

"How long will Mom have to be gone?" Beege asked.

"It's hard to tell, Beege. As I told those people out in California, nobody gets well on schedule. The doctors think your mother may be on the brink of a nervous breakdown, but with plenty of rest and quiet, well—it may never happen. I really can't guess how long she'll have to be away. Maybe just a few weeks. Maybe a few months."

"A few months!" That came from me. I guess I shouldn't have sounded so spooked when I said it, for Migsy started to cry again and buried her head in Dad's shoulder. Dad held her away from him and looked at her. His eyes were kind, but stern. He looked at Beege and me the same way.

"Now stop the tears, Migs. And listen, all three of you. I don't want any sad, long faces around here. Leaving us is going to be very hard on your mother, and I want her to know that she's leaving a cheerful family behind. Aunt Ann is driving down from New York and will arrive some time tomorrow. She and Mom will leave here early Sunday morning. I want to see a lot of smiles around this house until then. Do you read me, boys? Do you understand, Migsy?"

We all nodded.

"Okay," Dad said. "Now let's finish our dinner and then clean up the kitchen so well that Mom will wonder why she ever worried about leaving us. Okay, Pooh Bear?"

"Okay," Migsy said, jumping off Dad's lap. That's one thing about little kids. Sometimes you can make them forget something just by pretending something else.

Dad looked relieved. I guess it was a hard thing for him to have to do, telling us about Mom, and he was glad it was over. The telling part was over, anyway. The rest of it was just beginning.

Nine

MOM LEFT with Aunt Ann early Sunday morning. She was holding out okay until just about the last minute, but she started to cry when she was getting into the car. Then Migsy started to cry, and, well, it was pretty awful.

Dad got us busy right away getting ready for church. He said life was going to go on, and that the best thing we could do for Mom was to have our lives be just as they always were even with her away. That meant not missing church. Dad was right. When you're busy doing something, you're probably not going to be sitting around getting messed up with a lot of thinking. Church was a good thing to do.

I wondered if I was going to pray about Mom,

though. I'm not much on praying. I guess I just don't know how. Also, I sometimes get a little scared about it. I mean, supposing I prayed and asked God to make Mom well and then she never got well. How would I feel about God?

Take for instance when I was a little guy and asked Santa Claus for an egg that would hatch a live dinosaur, and then all I got was a crummy plastic egg that you opened up and inside was this stuffed duck. I was so mad at Santa Claus that I wouldn't have stopped to help him if he'd had a flat reindeer on the North Pole freeway.

I like God. I don't want to be mad at him. So I think a lot about praying.

When we're kneeling to pray in church, I look around at the family. Beege and Micky and Dad all pray the same way with their hands folded and their heads bent down and their eyes closed. They always look nice and peaceful. So does Mom except that she folds her hands and puts them up to her eyes. They really look like they know what they're doing. Migsy screws her eyes tight shut and then screws up her nose and practically her ears too. Then she grabs the pew in front of her like she was about to take off and fly up to heaven if she didn't. Boy, you just know Migsy's praying like crazy.

I personally close my eyes for about three seconds and then, because I don't know what I'm doing, I open them again. I usually end up staring at the neck of some lady in front of me who has this dress zipper that isn't zipped up to the top. I always worry about whether I should reach over and zip up the zipper, only I never do it. The lady would probably turn around and sock me.

112

Anyway, I don't remember whether I prayed or not that day. Maybe I did a little. When you do just a little and don't make the big deal out of it, you don't get so mad when it doesn't happen. I've found that out.

When we got home, Migsy and I set to work on Glorious' new home in the basement. It gave us something to do to help forget about Mom. The only thing was that I didn't have one crummy idea about how I was going to manufacture a pond in the basement.

At first I just thought we'd put the stopper in the laundry tub and fill it up with water and a few rocks. Dad wrecked that plan. He reminded me that we'd have to remove Glorious every time we ran the washing machine, and if we ever forgot, we'd end up with one boiled frog.

My second plan was to bring in some of the rocks that both the state of Virginia and our own backyard are filled with and stick them all together with cement. I thought about it pretty carefully and couldn't see anything dangerous to Glorious in the plan. So I informed Migsy about it, and we started bringing in rocks. After we had about all the rocks that we needed, I found a bag of cement powder that Dad had and read the directions. It didn't sound like much of a deal, mixing it with sand and all, so I found a tin bucket and, after telling Migsy that she'd better not get her hands in it and should leave it to the experts, I started pouring.

I hadn't poured very far before Dad appeared. He asked what I thought I was doing. I informed him that I was about to mix up some cement. He informed me otherwise. He also informed me that I'd better have all those rocks out of the basement before I went to bed that night, or else. I didn't ask him or else *what*, because I had done that once and found out.

I had some trouble getting Migsy to help me carry out the rocks. She said it was my idea and she shouldn't have to. Then I reminded her that if she ever wanted an indoor home for Glorious she'd better. So she did. All this work kept us busy, and while you were working down in the basement, you could almost forget that Mom wasn't upstairs fixing Sunday dinner or baking cookies or even just reading the Sunday paper and having coffee with Dad. Not quite forget it, but almost.

I suddenly noticed, though, that nobody had reminded Migsy to take off her Sunday dress and put on her playclothes. "Boy, Migsy, Mom's going to have something to say about that. You're a mess," I said.

Migsy looked down at herself. The next thing I knew, she was picking at her dress and her lower lip had started to quiver. Migsy loves her red velvet dress like it was her own skin. Then I opened my big mouth even farther.

"Hey, I just thought of something funny, Migs. Mom can't say anything because she isn't even here. How about that? You can get as dirty as you want!" On top of reminding her that her favorite dress was all messed up, I had now reminded her that Mom was gone. Migsy really started to sniffle then.

"Look, Migsy, quit it," I said. "I'm sorry. Hey, your dress isn't that bad. Honest! And Mom's going to be back before you know it. Listen, I've got another neat idea for a home for Glorious."

Migsy stopped crying and looked at me with her big blue eyes wide open and her long eyelashes practically glued to her forehead, waiting for this big idea of mine. Which I didn't happen to have.

I started walking slowly around the basement, pretending to be mysterious and peering at all our old trunks and boxes and all the junk we had stacked up. I could tell that Migsy was interested in my performance and had practically forgotten all about her dress and Mom being gone and everything else. I guess I must have been praying then. At least I was sure as heck talking to *someone*, asking for an idea in a hurry. Migsy must have thought I'd lost a few marbles when I suddenly looked up to the basement ceiling and said, "Thanks!"

What had happened was that I'd seen this piece of blue plastic stuff with yellow ducks all over it, sticking out from between two of Dad's wooden footlockers. "Aha, exactly what I was looking for," I announced to Migsy.

"What is it? What is it?"

"No less than a new home for Glorious," I said, pulling out the plastic and shaking it open.

"That's my old wading pool," Migsy said. "Is that what you were looking for, Andrew?"

"Absolutely," I said, hoping I wouldn't get struck dead for lying. "I'll bet the Smithsonian couldn't come up with a better idea for a frog—a real, genuine plastic frog pool blown up by the personal air of Andrew Kellogg."

Migsy liked the wading-pool idea, but the trouble was that the personal air of Andrew Kellogg wasn't enough to blow it up. After practically turning blue in the process, I ended up having to dig around in Beege's precious box of stuff and borrow his basketball pump. Then Migsy and I dragged a few rocks back in from the yard and put them in the middle, so Glorious would have a hill to sit on. Finally we filled the pool with water to see how it looked. It looked great. We even tried Glorious out in it for a while, and he didn't get any big ideas about getting out. I really felt like the big deal, not just for getting the pool fixed up, but for getting Migsy's mind off Mom for a while.

Then Beege had to appear.

"What's the big idea of messing around with my gear?" he asked me the minute he set foot in the basement. He's got radar for any time I touch any of his stuff. "Who told you you could use my pump?"

"Beege, we were just using it to blow up the pool for Glorious," I said. "Besides, you said you were going to help us, so I didn't think you'd mind."

"Well, I do, and I don't want you laying your grimy paws on my things again. And look at the mess you've made. You'd better get this cleaned up. Boy, Andrew, Mom isn't gone for five minutes and you're messing everything up."

The big crumb! He'd never worried about messes and dirt and stuff like that in his whole life before. You should have seen his room. I wouldn't have kept a pig in it.

I looked over at Migsy, and I could see that she was starting to puddle up again. But Beege stomped out of there on his big feet and never even saw what he'd done to Migsy. He acted like he was practically God or something now that Micky wasn't around anymore. All he did was look back from the stairs and say, "Get busy!" I stood there wishing I was big enough to clobber him.

It was a good thing I'd forgotten one thing we still had to arrange for Glorious, and that was how we were going to keep him warm enough down in the basement. By the time we'd found this crazy old gooseneck lamp and a table to put it on, found a plug and moved the pool over to it, Migsy was all happy again about Frog Paradise, which is what we decided to call it.

We got through the rest of Sunday pretty well, all things considered. Dad took us out to a Hot Shoppe for dinner and then let us stay up extra late looking at the movie on television. We picked up some postcards when we were at dinner, and we all wrote to Mom that night, too. I'm not much at writing letters, but Dad said that just seeing our handwriting would help Mom. My handwriting would set someone back about ten years, but I decided not to mention it. Beege would have had something beautiful to say about it, and I didn't want to hear any more of his crummy philosophy.

The only thing was that just before we went to bed we all had some of the chocolate-chip cookies that Mom had finally baked for us. She bakes the best chocolate-chip cookies in the whole world. It made me sad, though, eating them that night.

The next day we got Josie. Josie was the lady Mom had hired to look after us while she was gone. I guess Dad had said we didn't need anyone, but Mom said she wouldn't leave unless they hired a lady to come in at least part time, especially in the afternoons after school. Who, she asked, was going to take care of Migsy between the time she got home and Dad got home from work? Beege certainly couldn't give up his football and basketball and guitar teaching. And as for Andrew, well!

It made me sick. With Beege, it was that you could hardly ask him to give up being the big deal even for an emergency, but with me, it was Andrew, well! I wished they'd quit using those unfinished sentences where I was concerned. I felt like a private national disaster or something. I didn't want to upset Mom with any remarks, though, so I kept my mouth shut.

But I have to tell you that I started thinking again about running away from home and enlisting or something like that and becoming the big deal hero. I mean, what chance did a guy like me have anywhere around home? But how could you run away from home when your mom was sick? Besides, I still had Robert E. Lee's Chinese descendants to think about. I could see my family standing there with tears in their eyes watching me getting my F.B.I. medal for uncovering this huge plot to start up the Civil War again. That would be the last time they'd wonder if I was able to do a little thing like look after Migsy. Except Beege. He wouldn't cry over me if I was a crummy corpse.

Anyway, about Josie. I didn't think I'd like someone trying to take Mom's place, telling us what to do and all that. But you couldn't help liking Josie.

Dad told us we were to call Josie Mrs. Edwards, but she said she wouldn't hear us if we did. So we called her Josie. She was just the right person to jolly us along, as she called it, and you should have heard her laugh, especially at the stuff Migsy said. This was great for Migsy.

I had to get used to being called honey, though. Josie called everyone honey. Except for Dad.

No one could be Mom, but if we had to have someone, it was a good thing it was Josie.

Migsy came charging up to my room one day. "Hey, Andrew! Andrew! Guess what?"

"You lost another tooth," I said.

"Oh no, Andrew. Guess what? Guess what?"

"I've already guessed. You tell me what."

Migsy plunked down on my bed. "Diane says there's a crazy lady living right around the corner!"

"You don't say. How does Diane know so much about it?"

"Arthur told her."

"Oh, him!" I turned around toward my desk and started looking at my book again.

"It's true. Diane even showed me the house where she lives. So there!"

"Okay. So Diane showed you the house where this crazy lady lives. So what about it?"

"I'm scared."

"Oh, for Pete's sake, Migsy! Don't go believing everything Diane tells you. There's no crazy lady living around here. I'll bet there isn't."

"There is, too! I can show you the house right where she lives. It's near us. I'm scared."

"Migsy, you don't have to show me the house. I already know which one it is. It's Sally Ardery's house, isn't it?"

Migsy gave me a funny look, and nodded.

"So who's the crazy lady?" I asked. "Is Sally supposed to be the crazy lady?"

"No. It's her mommy."

"Have you ever seen her mother?" I asked.

"No."

"Well, I have," I said. Migsy looked at me as if she'd swallowed a wad of bubble gum. "I met her last Friday. She isn't any crazier than you are."

"Well, Diane says that Arthur says that Sally's mommy goes to a place called a sani—sani—well, to a place. She goes there because she's crazy."

"Look, Migsy, Mrs. Ardery goes to a sanitarium. She goes because she's sick. Maybe the sickness has something to do with her head, but for Pete's sake, Migsy, sick is sick. Like sick to your stomach or your toe or anyplace else. You don't go around making crummy remarks about people who have stomachaches, do you? What's the big idea of doing it when someone has a little problem with his head? That Arthur is a rotten crumb. And don't you listen to what Diane says anymore. Okay?"

"Okay," Migsy said, but she didn't look too sure about it.

I was feeling pretty sick myself, thinking about our own mom. Maybe Mom wasn't going to any sanitarium, but she was going away for a rest, whatever that meant. Supposing that lousy Arthur Kogel said something to Migsy about *Mom* being crazy. I just knew that if that rotten guy ever said anything to *me* about her, I'd kill him. I *thought* I would anyway. You can't count on a thing like that when you're a rotten, lousy chicken, especially when he's got this overgrown behemoth named Melvin Funkhauser hanging around him half the time.

Even though I didn't give them another chance to arrange a big deal for practically ending my life, they never gave up on me. It looked like they'd formed this organization just to make my life miserable. L. G. K.—*Let's Get Kellogg.* I kept wondering why those twin crumbs couldn't think of anything better to do with themselves. You can imagine, then, what a pleasant surprise it was to my personal self when the organization busted up. Maybe it's only what you'd call temporary and the creeps will get back together again. But for now they've busted up, and I was around when it happened.

I'd taken Grover for a walk, and we ended up near Migsy's school. At the back of her school playground is a grove of trees and tall evergreen hedges. Grover and I were going to cut across it when we came near one of the hedges and heard these voices coming from behind it.

You can tell whether voices are friendly even if you can't hear the words, and these weren't exactly carrying on a friendly conversation. I slowed Grover down and crept up on the hedge. Through it I saw these two guys, and they were fighting, all right. Grover started to growl, but they were too busy to hear him. I told Grover to be quiet or else, and he was. The two guys were Arthur Kogel and Melvin Funkhauser.

"I told you to shut up about my parents!" Arthur shouted. His face was bright red.

"What did I say? What did I say?" Melvin said.

"You know what you said!"

"Well, so what if I did? It's true, isn't it? Aren't they getting a divorce and each one is turning right around and marrying someone else?"

"So what if they are!"

"So they're some kind of parents, running around like that. Sheesh!"

"You shut your damn mouth about my parents!" Arthur screamed. He looked like he was about to cry.

"Just who do you think you're swearing at?"

"I'll swear at anybody I like!"

"Well, you'd better not swear at me. Jerk!"

"Try and stop me!" Arthur yelled.

Through all this I was standing there like I'd been hypnotized. I couldn't believe what I was seeing and hearing.

The next thing I knew, Melvin had moved up to Arthur and swung his arm out at him. I could practically feel it landing on my eye. I don't know much about fighting. Nothing, you might say. But even I could see that Arthur wasn't much in that department. He swung back at Melvin, only the swing went wide. It probably wouldn't have done much if it had landed anyway. It took Melvin about two seconds to land Arthur on his back. Then he was down on top of Arthur, beating him to pieces. Arthur just lay there like an overturned turtle waving his flippers around. He was crying and sniveling.

Melvin finally stood up. "Don't you ever open your big, fat mouth to swear at me again!" He started to walk off toward the school playground. Then he turned once more and yelled back, "Creep!"

Arthur rolled over onto his stomach and threw his head down on his arms. He was sobbing. I didn't know what to do, but I finally decided the best thing was to leave. Arthur wasn't killed or anything, so I didn't feel crummy about leaving him.

The next day, Arthur and Melvin didn't sit together on the bus. They weren't together anyplace. I couldn't believe it had happened, but I felt funny about it just the same. Especially hearing that stuff about Arthur's parents. I'd never met them, but once in a while on my way to the bus I'd seen them getting into their cars in the morning to go to work. They both work, I found out. Migsy said that Diane said that sometimes they'd have to work all night and never come home until morning. They must have some kind of funny jobs. They must be some kind of funny parents. I agree with what Melvin said to Arthur. I have to be honest. But still you shouldn't go around telling people what you think of their crummy parents. You just shouldn't do that.

Anyway, Arthur and Melvin haven't been seen together since.

Ten

FOR A COUPLE of days, about all I did was go around congratulating myself on all the sudden freedom from agony. I couldn't stop thinking, though, about how it had happened, especially the part about Arthur's mom and dad. I wondered how it would feel if that ever happened in our family.

Then something did happen in our family that put the whole thing right out of my mind. Dad found out he had to go on a trip to Europe. He'd known about it for a long time, but he kept thinking the trip would be canceled. It wasn't. He was really worried about it, about leaving us kids and at the same time knowing that all the meetings he had to attend were important and he should be there. If it hadn't been for our already having Josie, and everything in the house running like a clock with new batteries, I don't know what he would have done.

"What did Mom say when you called her?" Beege asked Dad as Josie was serving us dinner the night before he left.

"She was all ready to pack up and come back, naturally. But I think I finally convinced her that Josie had everything under control and that you kids were happy. It was a tough fight, but I won it. Now, I want it understood that you're all to mind Josie and not give her any kind of hard time. You hear that, Josie?"

"I hear it, Mr. Kellogg," said Josie.

"And I'm leaving a detailed itinerary here, and instructions that Josie's to call or wire me if there's any trouble at all. Is that understood?"

"Mr. Kellogg, there isn't going to be any trouble. You just leave everything to me," Josie said.

"Heck, Dad, we'll be fine," Beege said. "We'll make out. You don't have to worry about a thing." Good old Beege! You could figure on *him* not worrying.

"Thanks, Beege," Dad said. "I'm counting on you to help Josie out. But you remember that I'll still be concerned about you. After all, you're sixteen and hopefully responsible. But Migsy here is only six."

"Going on seven next week, Daddy," Migsy said. "Daddy! You won't be here for my birthday!"

"I'm sorry about that, Piglet, but I've talked to Josie, and I'm sure she'll see that you have a good celebration."

"Will I have a party?"

"You sure will, honey, a real nice party," Josie said.

"But as I was saying, Beege, Migsy is only six going

on seven." Dad stopped a moment and then gave what sounded a lot to me like a big sigh. "And, of course, Andrew!"

And of course Andrew *what?* What did he mean by that? Well, I knew what he meant. Maybe I didn't blame him for thinking that way when you considered how I was always messing things up. But did he have to say it? I might have started a discussion about it, but what would have been the use? A crummy kid was a crummy kid. How could you argue it?

Anyway, Dad said he'd be gone at least two weeks, maybe right up until Christmas. It wasn't a very beautiful prospect, but I told Migsy if she went around looking droopy I'd clobber her.

It was okay right after Dad left, original and all that, not having Mom and Dad around to tell us what to do. But then we had Josie. She stayed until eight o'clock every night to get Migsy to bed, and then she was back again first thing in the morning to get us breakfast. I guess she would have just stayed with us while Dad was gone except that her husband is dead, and she has these two kids at home. The boy is grown-up, but the girl is in high school, so Josie had to get home to see that everything was okay with her.

Then one morning just a few days after Dad left, Josie didn't show up. Migsy was practically hysterical.

"Look," I said as I was fixing us up some cornflakes, "her son's car probably broke down. She'll be here when you get home from school. I swear it, Migsy."

Migsy didn't look too convinced.

Then Beege walked into the kitchen, rubbing his eyes. "Hey, what's up? Where's Josie?"

"She's not here yet. I guess she's late. I've been try-ing to tell Migsy that Frank probably had car trouble or something, but she doesn't believe me."

"Sure she'll be here," Beege said. "Cheer up, Migsy." Migsy cheered up right away. Just one word from Beege, like he was a Roman oracle or something. "What's for breakfast?" Beege asked, peering over my shoulder.

"Cornflakes," I said.

"Very well, I'll have some," said Beege.

I should have told him to pour his own lousy corn-flakes, but I didn't. I got out another bowl and fixed him some.

Josie still wasn't there when I got home from school. I knew it right away because Migsy was sitting on the front steps and Grover was still in the backyard where I'd left him. He was so glad to see me I knew he'd been alone all day.

Josie hadn't shown up by dinnertime either. She doesn't have a telephone, so we couldn't call her, but about five-thirty *our* telephone rang. It was Beege saying he wouldn't be home for dinner. He asked me if Josie was there and I said no.

"Oh brother!" Beege said. "Look, I'm over at Mike Roney's house. They've asked me for dinner but, look, maybe I'd better come home."

"No, that's okay," I said.

"You sure?"

"Oh sure," I said, not feeling too sure about anything.

"Is Migsy okay?"

"Yeah, she's fine."

"Can you fix something to eat?"

"Oh sure," I said.

"Well, I'll get home as soon as I can. If Josie doesn't show, we'll talk about it then. Sure you're okay?"

"Oh sure," I said.

"See ya, then," said Beege.

"See ya," I said.

So that was that. It looked like it was going to be a beautiful evening. Migsy and I had to eat, though, so I opened a can of corned beef and a can of sardines and a bottle of stuffed olives, and after I'd said the blessing, we had it with graham crackers and milk. Then I made Migsy take a vitamin pill in case I'd forgotten anything.

After that, Migsy looked at television while I did my homework. Then we both looked at television until I saw that it was time for Migsy to get to bed.

"I'm not going," Migsy said.

"What do you mean you're not going?" I asked.

"I'm going to wait for Josie."

"Well, Josie isn't—I mean, how do we know what time Josie will get here? Maybe not until tomorrow morning. Are you going to stay up until tomorrow morning?"

"Then I'll wait for Beege."

"Beege may not get home until—until twelve o'clock. Look, Migsy, we happen to have Dad's itinerary, which is, for your information, something that tells where he is at every minute of every day. Now, I can telephone him. Or on second thought, maybe I'd better just clobber you."

Migsy went into her big thinking act. It's true that she can beat me at tiddlywinks, but I'm still bigger than she is. "Okay," she said finally, "I guess I'll go to bed."

"Very well," I said. And then I added in a pretty icy tone, "Please call me if you wish me to turn out your light."

Migsy was halfway up the stairs when she called back. Her voice sounded small and sad. "Who's going to hear me say my prayers?"

"Well, around the house there happens to be one dog and one frog and me," I said, still pretty haughty. "Whom did you have in mind?"

More thinking from Migsy and then in an even smaller voice, "Will you?"

"Oh sure," I said. Heck, I'm always willing to let bygones be bygones. "Let me know when you're ready."

"Do I have to have a bath?"

"Do you feel dirty?" I asked. I personally don't believe in baths unless you feel dirty.

"No," said Migsy.

"Okay, you can skip it," I said.

Migsy hopped on up the stairs, and for a few minutes I didn't feel so gloomy, playing the big deal grown-up and all that. The feeling didn't last very long, though. A house at night is when you can really tell you're alone. I wondered if we'd ever hear from Josie again. I couldn't believe that she'd desert us without saying anything. You hear a lot about this kind of stuff happening, people with no loyalty and all that, but it's always about people you don't know, so you don't care. I wished Beege would get home.

I knew I'd better not let Migsy know how I felt about everything, or she'd get all shook up again. When she called to me that she was ready, I tried to think that it wasn't just us alone in the house. I turned on all the lights downstairs, though.

Migsy was kneeling by her bed all ready to go with the prayers when I got there. She just kills me. She really does, in her pink nightgown with the lacy stuff around the neck. She looks like this one picture in a book Mom has from when she was a little girl.

"Okay, you may commence," I said.

"You have to kneel down with me," said Migsy.

"What do you mean, kneel down with you? I'm not doing the praying, am I?"

"Mommy and Daddy and Josie kneel down with me," Migsy said. "You have to kneel down with me." She squeezed her lips together so her mouth looked like a little thin pencil. I didn't want any arguments about Migsy praying, for Pete's sake, so I knelt down. Migsy closed her eyes tight and screwed up her face just like she does in church. Then she grabbed tight onto her bed and started in the "Now I lay me down to sleep."

Besides being this great prayer, Migsy is a great blesser. She blessed just about everything in the whole world, Mom and Dad and Micky and Beege and me and Grandma and Grandpa, then Miss Pinkley, her teacher, and all the kids in her class and her Sunday School class, and Grover and Glorious and even his mealworms. Then she blessed her teddy bear and her stuffed elephant and all her dolls and practically every toy she owns. After that she started in on stuff like her room and the cherry-flavored cough syrup, Dad's electric razor and the waffle iron, and even the television set. I tell you, I lost track of all the stuff Migsy was blessing.

My knees went numb. I started to grab the bed myself just to keep from falling over. I'd practically stopped even listening. Suddenly Migsy stopped, looked over at me with one eye open, and said, "Do you think I ought to bless Josie?"

"Sure you ought to bless Josie," I said. "Why wouldn't you?"

"Isn't Josie bad?" Migsy asked.

I wished someone else was around. I'm not much on religion and philosophy and that kind of stuff. I mean, what does a guy know who doesn't even know about praying, for Pete's sake? I sure didn't want to steer Migsy wrong.

"Look, you blessed the TV set, didn't you?"

"Yes."

"Well, boyoboy, that goes bad all the time. Do you stop blessing it when it goes bad?"

"No."

"So bless Josie. Besides, who said Josie was bad anyway?"

"God bless Josie," said Migsy. "And please make her well again. Amen. I've already brushed my teeth. See?"

"Very good," I said. "Now, get into bed." I have to be honest. I'd forgotten all about brushing teeth, but you don't want to admit anything like that when you're in charge. I tucked the blankets in and patted Migsy on the head. Then I turned out the light. Just as I was leaving the room, though, something suddenly struck me.

"Migsy, what did you mean, 'please make her well again'?"

"Josie said last night she didn't feel good. She had a tummy ache."

"How come you never mentioned it before?"

"I just remembered."

"Boy, Migsy, you ought to remember stuff like that," I said.

"Why?"

"Because maybe Josie is sick. Maybe that's why she isn't here today."

"Why didn't she call us, then?"

"I don't know," I said, and I didn't. She could have had Geraldine, her daughter, call from school, or Frank call from work. I finally decided that what Migsy had just said really didn't make any difference anyway.

"Well, go to sleep," I said. "Good night."

"Good night."

I didn't quite make it to the stairway.

"Andrew!"

I turned and went back to Migsy's room. "What?"

"Diane says babies come in alligator handbags. Do they?"

"Who told Diane a dumb, stupid thing like that?" I asked.

"Her mother told her once."

"Look, Migsy, I thought I told you not to listen to what Diane says anymore. Now, you just go to sleep."

"Okay," Migsy said.

I started for the stairs again. Boy, I was telling myself, I'd personally never been a mother, but if I was I'd never tell my kid a dumb thing like that. An alligator handbag! Sheesh!

"Andrew!"

I gave a big sigh and headed back to Migsy's room. "What this time?"

"Andrew, where *do* babies come from?"

Silence from me.

"Andrew?"

"I'm thinking," I said.

"Don't you know?"

"Sure I know!"

"Then where do they?"

"Well, I'll tell you one thing," I said. "I'll tell you this—boy, Migsy, they sure don't come in alligator handbags!"

"Oh," said Migsy, "okay."

I practically staggered back to the stairs. Migsy never gives up that easily.

"Andrew!"

I thought I'd faint. I mean, I'm personally just not prepared to give lectures on the kind of stuff Migsy was talking about. If Migsy didn't shut up, I was going to have to clobber her, and that was all.

"Look, Migsy," I said, sounding pretty mean, "you'd better go to sleep. I'm not going to answer any more junk. I mean it!"

There was no answer from Migsy. Then I heard this little sniffle from over where the bed was. I was ready to kill myself. Here was this teeny, tiny kid, and her mom was sick, and her dad was gone, and Josie hadn't shown up and all that.

"Hey, Migsy, I'm sorry," I said. "Look, you can have one more question." I braced myself against the door, expecting the worst.

"Andrew, if Josie doesn't come tomorrow, who's going to have my birthday party?"

I nearly died with relief. On the other hand, remembering Migsy's birthday party wasn't very good news. I'd forgotten all about it. Not that I hadn't already gotten her a present, because I had. It was a bunch of stuff for Glorious, more mealworms, a little diving guy that shoots up bubbles, a couple of glass mermaids, and a package of colored rocks. Micky had sent something, and she had boxes from Beege and Mom and Dad. Presents weren't the problem, but the party was. I just couldn't clobber Migsy with any more bad news.

"Look, Migsy, if Josie doesn't come, *I'll* give you your birthday party."

"Will Beege, too?"

"Sure Beege will," I said, thinking to myself that Beege had better.

"Will I have my favorite cake and everything?"

"Sure you will. Now go to sleep. Okay?"

"Okay," Migsy said.

What was I doing promising Migsy her favorite cake? Beege and I could probably manage the party since she'd only invited six little girls. We could buy ice cream and lemonade, but where could we buy the kind of cake Migsy wanted? It's a cake with this terrible icing that has strawberry jam in it. Mom made it once by mistake, and now Migsy has to have it every birthday. I felt sunk.

I went to the kitchen to think things over and to help myself to a glass of milk and a couple of leftover sardines. That was when I decided that if Migsy was ever going to have her cake, it would have to be made by yours truly, Andrew Kellogg. And furthermore, it would have to be made right then, because there'd be no time after school before the party the next day. Before I had time to start in talking things over with myself and changing my mind, I began to figure just how I'd make the cake.

I told you before about our goofy kitchen. Well, I

didn't know just how goofy it was until I had to work in it. If Mom didn't have any other problems, this kitchen would have made her sick. It took me ten minutes just to decide where a cookbook would be kept. I finally found it, but not before I'd opened the wrong cupboard and the breadboard had fallen on my head.

I was already pretty dizzy from this when I turned to the cake section of Mom's cookbook. Even when you're not dizzy, the first thing you learn to cook shouldn't be a cake. I mean, at least not until you've been to a code school. I found a recipe that Mom called "Migsy's Birthday Cake." Under it was stuff like two and three-quarters tsp. BP, one half c. short., and one half T. grtd. lem. pl. I nearly collapsed with relief when I found that underneath it, good old Mom had written, "Or may use yellow cake mix."

So, after only a couple of minor accidents like practically gouging my eye out with the can opener and smashing my thumb in a drawer that shuts as if it had just been greased, I found three boxes of yellow cake mix and helped myself to one of them. Then I actually baked a cake with it. I know that any idiot can make a cake-mix cake, but when the idiot is twelve years old and a guy, I think it's pretty neat. While the cake was baking, I messed around making the icing.

The recipe said to use one box powdered sugar, one stick butter, and one jar strawberry jam, so I got out another bowl and threw in the sugar and the butter. All I could find in the jam department, though, was this one-quart jar of strawberry jam. It looked like a heck of a lot of jam, but the recipe said to use one jar, so I tossed it in.

I mean, except for the jar. Then I mixed it all up. What I ended up with was strawberry soup.

By the time I got through, I'd added another whole box of powdered sugar to the icing and it was still running all over the place. I had to stop adding stuff, though, because there was so much icing by then that I couldn't find a bowl big enough to mix it up in. No kidding. There was enough strawberry-jam icing to float an aircraft carrier.

I sure wasn't going to waste all those valuable ingredients, so I put the cake in this big baking pan of Mom's that has a high edge around it and poured all the icing over it. It slid right off, and the cake ended up looking like a volcanic island in the middle of a sea of strawberry lava. It would have been pretty fascinating if it hadn't been so sickening at the same time.

Just then the telephone rang. I was pretty sure it was Beege calling to tell me he was going to be late, as if he wasn't already, so I took my own pleasant time getting to the telephone. But it wasn't Beege. It was Geraldine, Josie's daughter, and she was talking so fast I could hardly understand her.

She was calling from the hospital. Josie had been taken there the night before with a ruptured appendix. This was the first time Geraldine and Frank had been able to see her since the operation. Geraldine was pretty scared. I could tell that. But she said her mom was going to be okay, and that was the main thing.

I felt terrible about Josie being sick. But I was happier about knowing that she hadn't deserted us. I guess I really knew she hadn't all along, but it's pretty hard to believe something like that when the only person telling you about it is yourself.

Geraldine explained why no one had called us. She had thought Frank was going to, and Frank had thought she was going to. So nobody did. I don't blame them, being so upset about their mom and all that. Geraldine said that Josie really pinned their ears back, though. Also she wanted to know what we were going to do without her, what we were going to do about Migsy's birthday party, and what we were going to do about calling Dad.

I didn't tell Geraldine about the strawberry disaster in the kitchen, but I told her to tell Josie we'd be okay and that Migsy would have her party. I kept my mouth shut about calling Dad.

After the phone call, I looked at the cake again. It didn't look like a volcano anymore, more like something sinking into a pink swamp. But I didn't care. After I'd heard about Josie, the cake looked practically edible. I finally got around to tasting the icing. Not bad. Not bad at all! I put some in a cup, took along a couple of sardines, grabbed another glass of milk, and went to look at the late show on TV until Beege got home.

Eleven

BEEGE finally came home. Late. He was pretty apologetic. I have to be honest. He didn't even make one of his beautiful remarks about my cake even though I could tell from his look what he was thinking.

Sitting in the kitchen, having glasses of milk, Beege and I discussed everything. We both agreed that we ought to try to handle the situation ourselves without calling Mom or Dad. Dad had left enough money with Beege so we didn't have to worry about that. Beege said we could probably manage Migsy, all right, the two of us together.

It was pretty neat, sitting there talking things over with Beege. I even began to think things weren't going to be too bad, and maybe Beege and I would . . .

Well, anyway, Beege wasn't too happy that I'd promised Migsy her party the next day. The thing was that he'd picked up a new guitar student. Not that he needed any more with all the ones he already had. This one's name was Angela. It didn't take me long to figure that she was more than just a guitar student. Still, he promised that he'd get the lesson over with right after school and get home by four for the party. I should have read the handwriting on the wall. The only thing is that I've never learned to read this ancient language called "boloney."

At four the next afternoon the party started, and naturally, there was no Beege. I didn't have time to get mad at him, though, because Migsy and her girl friends were waiting for me to start something. The little girls were all pretty polite, and I didn't have to clobber anybody. The thing that worried me, though, was that one of them would go home and blab that there was no grown-up running the show. So I clued Migsy in to tell anybody who asked that I was in charge because she'd asked Mom if I could be. Then I finally decided I didn't have to worry. Usually when you ask teeny kids if they've had a good time at a party, they just say "uh-huh" and then shut up. They never tell you anything. Unless they win a prize.

The only thing I had any real trouble with was games. You have to plan about fifty games for a little kid's party, and I didn't have one after Pin the Tail. So we played lots of drops. That's these games where you drop stuff. I had them drop beans into a milk bottle, and clothespins into a cottage-cheese box, and hair pins into a flowerpot, and macaroni into a mayonnaise jar (a clean one), and some other stuff I've forgotten. For prizes, I let them keep the stuff they'd dropped. They were crummy prizes, but the little girls didn't seem to mind. Even Diane Kogel acted pretty decent.

Maybe this was because of what I was having them pretend. I'd told the little kids that we'd been shipwrecked on this desert island, and whoever did the best pretending was going to be queen of the island. I did this mostly because of the refreshments. I mean, since Beege didn't show up, we never had any lemonade or ice cream. I felt sunk until I came up with the shipwreck idea. We had one lemon in the house, so I squeezed this into a pitcher and then added a bunch of sugar and some of Mom's red food coloring and a lot of water. I told the kids that this was liquid from the magic fountain and it didn't have much taste because magic liquid never does. One girl said it tasted a little like lemon, and I told her she got fifty points for being a good pretender. After that everybody tasted a little lemon, so they all got fifty points.

The big thing, though, was the cake. I told them it was a strawberry volcano that had just erupted because I'd lit Migsy's birthday candles. One kid said her mouth was burning from the strawberry lava, and then everybody was burning. They were neat pretenders. I told them that they were all so good I couldn't choose one queen, so they'd all have to be queen. Then I made boat paper hats from some ancient magical shipwrecked newspapers and crowned everybody.

Migsy said it was the best party she'd ever had. Some of the little girls said it was the best party they'd ever been to, and Migsy gave me this special blessing in her prayers that night.

I would have felt pretty good if it hadn't been for Beege. He'd telephoned at four-thirty to say he'd be a little late, and he didn't get home until five-thirty when the last guest was leaving. That made two nights running for him. It wasn't that I minded taking care of Migsy. It was just that Beege never said thanks or anything. I figured I'd never be the big deal with him if I lived until I was three million years old.

The next night Beege gave me a pretty good idea of how much he thought about my welfare. He'd been late again, but he was home about nine-thirty when the telephone rang. I thought maybe it was Mom calling, and I practically broke my neck getting there. It wasn't Mom, but the call *was* for me. It was Mr. Borne of the *Washington Star*. That's an evening paper that can be delivered after school. Mom and Dad had said that if a route opened up near enough with the *Star,* I could take it. Mr. Borne told me that a route had opened up, and our house happened to be almost in the middle of it. The only thing was that it was an emergency. Mr. Borne asked me if I could start right away. Boy, could I! I asked him to hold the phone a minute, because I thought I ought to check it out with Beege. I raced up to his room, but I could have saved the trip.

"I appreciate your problem, Andrew," said Beege, "but I just don't see how you can do it. Who's going to be here with Migsy? As it is, she waits in the house alone for half an hour until you get back from school. Look, I'd like to see you get the route, but you know I can't get out of basketball every day. And how about my guitar lessons? I couldn't guarantee I'd be here every day. It's impossible. Just tell the man to keep you on his list. I'm sorry."

"But, Beege," I said, "it'll be a million years before there's a route right around our neighborhood. Look, you said we'd both—I mean, that you'd help. Gee whiz, Beege!"

Beege banged a book down on his desk. "Andrew, I said forget it!" Then he picked up his pen and started in again on his homework. I knew the conversation had ended.

I stomped on down the hall for whatever good it would do. The crumb! The crumb! The big, fat, rotten, lousy crumb! "Like to see you get the route!" "Appreciate your problem!" My aching eyebrow! All he appreciated was himself.

I told Mr. Borne I guessed he'd have to get someone else and then went to my room. For about half an hour all I did was sit at my desk and chew the erasers off the tops of pencils.

It was ten o'clock before I started thinking about another problem I had to solve before I went to bed that night, my English theme. With Josie not showing up and Migsy's party on top of that, I was really late getting around to it. Now it was due the next day, and I didn't even have an idea.

It would have been better if I'd just turned in a blank piece of paper with my apologies. But I didn't. Maybe I felt I had to be the big deal with someone. With Mrs.

Carmichael. With anyone. I don't know why I did it. All I know is that I wrote a note at the top of the paper telling Mrs. Carmichael that what I was about to say was all private stuff. Then I began to write the theme.

You won't believe it, but the subject of that theme was the Chinese mansion and how I, Andrew S. Kellogg, super sleuth, had arrived at the conclusion that living in it were the glorious Chinese descendants of General Robert E. Lee!

Beege was true to his word about not being able to get out of basketball and his other stuff every day. Truer. He couldn't get out of it *any* day. He did manage to find the time to go grocery shopping with us, though. He even stayed around long enough to wash his own cereal bowl in the morning and once in a while make his own bed. But most of the time Migsy and I were on our own.

From what I could tell, she was holding up okay and not minding everything too much. Of course, Christmas was coming, and that was pretty helpful. Migsy was so excited thinking about it that she hardly had time to think about anything else.

Weekends are the worst without your mom or dad around. It was a good thing Migsy and I had only a couple of them left to fill before Dad was supposed to get back. Migs kept wanting to go into Washington to see all the Christmas stuff, but I didn't think Mom and Dad would like me taking her in, me being so undependable and all that. Good old Beege promised he would and then ended up not being able to. I forget his excuse.

When I found Migsy crying, I decided that no matter how undependable I was, I'd take her in to see Santa Claus and the Christmas trees in the Ellipse. I wasn't even going to ask Beege about it and get one of his big deal replies. I told Migs privately that I'd take her, but she'd have to wait until Christmas vacation started.

Tuesday night of the last week of school before Christmas vacation, I came down with this rotten cold, so I didn't go to school Wednesday and Thursday. Mom always makes us stay home when we have a cold, so Beege didn't say anything about it. Friday I went back.

On the bus, some of the seventh-grade kids looked at me in a kind of funny way, but I was used to it so I didn't pay much attention. I saw Arthur look at me, then over toward Melvin, then back at me. You could tell that Melvin saw Arthur, but he was so busy being friends with another guy that he never paid any attention to Arthur. Finally Arthur gave up.

Nothing much happened in homeroom either except one guy nudging another guy and saying in a low voice, "Hey, there's Kellogg. Let's give a round of applause to Kellogg. Wheee!" But that wasn't new either.

Then it was time for English. I'd just settled at my desk when Mrs. Carmichael looked up at me.

"Andrew, would you please come up here a moment. I have something for you."

I went up to her desk.

"Here," she said, handing me some papers clipped together. "I handed the themes back on Wednesday. If you don't mind, Andrew, I'd like to talk to you about this for a moment after class." I knew that it was my Robert E. Lee theme, because that was the only one Mrs.

Carmichael hadn't returned. There was a big red D written on the final sheet of the theme. My insides flipped. Boy, no wonder Mrs. Carmichael wanted to talk to me after class! But I couldn't figure out why she was smiling at me in such a kind way when she said it. Probably because she felt sorry for me. I don't mean about the D, but because I'd just made myself out the creep of the century.

I took another look at the D on my way back to my desk. Then I stopped, turned around, and went back up to Mrs. Carmichael. I guess my eyes were blinking in this funny way.

"Is something wrong, Andrew?" Mrs. Carmichael asked.

"This isn't my paper, Mrs. Carmichael," I said.

"Andrew, it must be. Yours was the only one I hadn't turned back, and that was because you were absent."

I held up the paper and pointed to the name in the upper right-hand corner of the front sheet. It was Arthur Kogel—written in handwriting about as crummy as mine. Arthur Kogel—Andrew Kellogg. Anybody could have read it wrong.

Mrs. Carmichael's face turned white. She put her hand up to her mouth and whispered, "Oh no! Oh, Andrew, I couldn't have been so careless!" The thing is, we both knew that she had, that she'd given Arthur *my* theme. Seeing Mrs. Carmichael's face made me wish Robert E. Lee had never been born, or me either. Especially me. I knew that if Arthur Kogel had read my theme, I was through.

"Class," Mrs. Carmichael said, "I believe there may have been some error made when I passed your themes back to you Wednesday. Arthur Kogel, would you please come up and get this one, which is yours. Did I hand you Andrew Kellogg's theme? And if so, would you please return it to me now?"

Arthur shuffled up to Mrs. Carmichael's desk. "I don't have it anymore," he said.

Mrs. Carmichael's eyes were shooting fireworks. I've never seen her mad like that before. "Well, Arthur, would you please explain why, if you had the theme in the first place, you didn't return it to me at once? Who *does* have it now, if *you* don't?"

Arthur just shrugged.

"I won't accept that. I'm asking you again, Arthur, to whom did you give Andrew's theme?"

"To Bill Culver," mumbled Arthur.

"You may return to your desk, Arthur. Bill, may I please have Andrew's theme?"

"I don't have it," Bill Culver said. "Marilyn Desilet has it."

Well, as it turned out, Marilyn Desilet didn't have it. Neither did John Simmons or Arny McMillan or Aaron Linneman or Genine Phister or twenty other people. It became pretty clear that practically the whole class had had a look at Andrew Kellogg's ideas on the Chinese descendants of Robert E. Lee.

It finally ended up that nobody in the class had the theme, but the last person whose miserable hands it had passed through was a girl named Roberta Vaughan. For all I knew then, my theme was at that moment the property of the whole Alexandria Public School System.

"And to whom did *you* give it?" Mrs. Carmichael snapped at Roberta.

Roberta looked around the room and giggled. It wasn't what you'd call a funny giggle, more like she was having a case of hysterics. "I gave it to—to Bobby Lee!"

"And who, may I ask, is Bobby Lee?" asked Mrs. Carmichael.

"He's the Chinese boy in Mr. Dirksen's room. His real name is Robert E. Lee the Third. His father works in Washington for the government. Bobby is the one that Andrew wrote . . ." Roberta gave another hysterical giggle. Another girl in the class giggled, too.

Mrs. Carmichael rapped on her desk. "That will be enough," she said. "Does anyone know where Bobby Lee is at this moment? In what class is he?"

Arny McMillan raised his hand. "He's in study period."

"Well, then, Arny, you may be excused to go and get that theme from Bobby Lee, assuming he still has it. Here is a slip to Miss Abrahams in study hall allowing you to speak to him. The rest of you will please open your English books to page thirty and study until Arny returns."

When Arny got back, Mrs. Carmichael practically snatched the theme out of his hand and gave it to me. Then she went back to her desk and turned to face the room. "Class, I don't ordinarily discuss any one student's work with all of you, and in this case I intend to make no exception. Since most of you have taken the liberty of reading Andrew Kellogg's theme, you already know the high mark it received and, therefore, what I think of it. Beyond this, I see no reason for me or for any of you to discuss this further either in or out of the classroom. I hope none of you will compound your guilt in this matter by doing so. A student's work is personal and private and should not be shared unless he wishes it. Frankly, I'm sorry and ashamed that this could have happened in my classroom. And now you will please continue studying until the bell rings. Arthur Kogel, will you please see me after school today?"

Mrs. Carmichael had done the best she could. But how was she going to know what went on after the kids left the classroom? I mean, how are you going to keep kids from whispering and sniggering and writing notes? And how are you going to keep kids from *thinking?*

When the bell rang, I must have been the first one up and out of that room. I hadn't forgotten that Mrs. Carmichael wanted to see me after class, but I had to get out of there. I couldn't stand to have all those kids staring at me even if my dashing out made Mrs. Carmichael think that I thought this was all her fault.

I shoved my way down the hall and into the boys' room. Then I headed for the last cubicle and closed myself into it. I stayed in that cubicle through all four lunch periods. A cubicle in a boys' room is a crummy place to spend your life. I stayed there, and I stayed there, and it seemed like about ten years before the last bell after the last lunch period rang, and everything got quiet. Then I sneaked out and on out of the school. I didn't care about missing my afternoon classes. I didn't care that I'd already come to school that day without an excuse for being absent. I didn't care about anything.

Once I was out, I didn't know what to do with myself, so I just walked around looking in shops and other places and not doing anything. I wasn't worried about the time, because Migsy had been invited to a friend's house to help trim a Christmas tree, and the people weren't bringing her home until after dinner. I had a whole afternoon full of time.

I spent a lot of it looking at the guinea pigs and white mice in the pet shop. Mice kill me the way they're always so busy doing nothing. Maybe that's because they only have a year to do it in. Turtles are the opposite. I mean, when you stop to think about it. After looking at the guinea pigs and the mice, I goofed around in the drugstore.

There are a couple of Christmas tree lots near the school, and I walked around looking at Christmas trees. I feel sorry for trees that have these skinny shapes. I always think we should buy trees like that until it comes right down to it. It's pretty sad. I counted all the skinny trees that day that probably no one would want and I counted nineteen.

It was starting to get dark then, and I headed for home. I didn't try to get the bus, though. I wanted to walk.

Most of the time when I come home from the bus, I don't go by Arthur Kogel's house. I go around the block. It's longer, but I don't want to take the chance of seeing him, with or without Melvin. I was pretty tired, though, by the time I got near home. It was cold, too, and I suddenly wanted to get home as fast as I could, even if there wouldn't be anyone there. I took the chance of going by Arthur's house.

"Well, if it isn't little teacher's pet!"

I don't know if Arthur had been waiting for me or what. It didn't matter. I just wanted to get past him.

149

This was pretty hard to do, though, because he was standing right in front of me.

"Hurrah for Cornflakes! Teacher thinks he has the cutest little imagination. Getting an A for making up a bunch of lies. Robert E. Lee's Chink descendants. Very amusing, Cornflakes."

I should have kept my big mouth closed, but I couldn't. "What do you mean 'Chink'? That's Chinese, for your information."

"Oh, Mr. Brilliant himself! Well, now, why don't you just run on home and write another theme. How about something on transients? Or here's a better one—a nice theme on *crazy* people. You should know all about that one. You could do a theme about your crazy mother!"

I'm not sure what happened after that. My mind tuned out, and I felt as if it wasn't even me standing there. My arm swung back, and I didn't come to until I felt my fist smacking up against Arthur's chest. Then something told me to duck, and I did. Arthur swung back at me, but his swing went wild. This time I knew what I was doing when I struck out at Arthur, and I hit something besides his chest. What I hit was his nose, and Arthur went right over on top of one of those gravestones he has all over his yard. He wasn't dead or anything, but he just lay there staring at me with a surprised, scared look on his face. There was enough light that I could see blood running down from his nose and into his mouth.

Before that, the only thing I'd ever smashed in my whole life was my own finger. I'd almost forgotten it. I won't forget about smashing someone's nose, though. There's all this gristle and stuff collapsing under your knuckles. Even if I could have done it, I didn't want to hit Arthur's nose again, but I stood there and waited for him to get up and come at me. He never did.

Suddenly I knew that Arthur was never going to get up and go on fighting. He'd probably lie there forever if I didn't leave. I guess I must have known from the time I saw Melvin beating up on Arthur what kind of guy he was. That he picked on me because I was a lot smaller than he was, and a lot punier, and I just plain looked chicken. I never gave him any reason to think anything else.

Now here he was lying on the ground with blood running out of his nose, probably waiting for me to jump on top of him and beat him up. I couldn't do it, though.

It wasn't because I was chicken. I swear it. I just didn't want to beat up on him. I mean, who'd want to smash someone who's lying there and staring at you with this big, scared face with blood running down from its nose? I hate Arthur Kogel, but I couldn't do it. I couldn't even yell something at him about his own crummy parents who were running around with other people and who probably taught him to say stuff like "Chink" and to call new people "transients" and sick people "crazy."

I just couldn't do it. I couldn't smash Arthur up any more. He was smashed enough already.

You know something? All your life you go around waiting for something to happen that will make you the big deal, and when it does, you muff it. One of the things I always thought would make me the biggest deal in the whole world was to beat up on a guy like Arthur until he was jelly, not just give him one sock and then quit. What

I did was reach into my coat pocket and pull out this handkerchief. It wasn't very clean, but it was all I had.

"Here," I said, holding it out, "use this."

Arthur rolled over on his side and went on wiping his bloody nose with the back of his hand.

"Take it," I said.

"Oh, dry up! Go away, why don't you?" Arthur said. He stumbled to his feet and went toward his house. Maybe he was just sniffing up blood. I couldn't tell, but it sounded like he was crying.

I stuffed the dirty handkerchief back into my pocket, pulled my coat collar up over my ears, and went home.

Twelve

THE NEXT day was Saturday, and I wasn't in the mood for anything, not even Christmas. But Migsy was. She was still begging to go into Washington to see Santa Claus and the Ellipse. Beege kept telling her that Dad would be back the next day and would be glad to take her. But I wasn't so sure. I didn't mean that Dad wouldn't do it, but that he wouldn't exactly be glad to. He's usually pretty tired after a trip. Sure, we could go Monday or even after Christmas, but Migs was dying to go Saturday, and besides all that, she woudn't let me forget that I'd *promised*. Little kids never let you forget when you've promised something.

Anyway, Beege went out in the afternoon. He had to give a couple of guitar lessons, and one of them was to this girl, Angela. He said he'd be back for dinner, but he'd said that a couple of dozen times before, and I knew just how early he'd be home. Especially after giving Angela a lesson.

So I ended up telling Migsy that I, Andrew, would personally escort her into Washington, and we bundled up and went.

I'd never gone into Washington on the bus, but we made out fine. I told the bus driver we wanted to go to Woody's, which is this big department store in Washington. "To see Santa Claus," Migsy told him. The driver was neat and told us exactly how to get there when we got off at the bus terminal on Pennsylvania Avenue, and we didn't get lost or anything stupid like that.

Migsy had brought her little purse with her and wanted to start right in with her Christmas shopping. I helped her to pick out powder for Mom and a golf ball for Dad. She got a ball-point pen for Micky so he'd write her a letter, and a date book for Beege. I thought the date book for Beege was pretty generous of Migsy, when you considered it. After that, I turned my back and Migsy bought my present, which was a bottle of shaving lotion. That isn't as funny as you'd think, because I told her that I'm considering taking up shaving.

My shopping didn't take long. Mom's gift was the hardest one to decide. I finally got her a picture frame for this picture Migsy had drawn of the family in crayon. Nobody looks like anybody in it, and Glorious is bigger than the whole family put together, but I knew Mom would like it. I had to pretend to buy Migsy a gift, though. I'd made her a wooden cradle for her doll. It was a little lopsided, but Migsy doesn't worry about stuff like that.

The thing that made me mad, though, was that I spent the most money on Beege. I got him this book on sports that he wanted. It cost a fortune. I don't know why I did it. I knew the crumb wouldn't even care that I spent practically my whole paltry savings on him.

Anyway, after we finished shopping, we went to see Santa Claus. Then we had hot dogs and chocolate sundaes at the fountain in the basement.

It was pretty late afternoon by then, and I figured we ought to get going if we were planning on making the Ellipse, which Migsy *was*. So I made a couple of inquiries, and we managed to find the right bus and get there.

Boy, it was neat! We must have gone around about a million times looking at the Christmas trees for all the states with the blue and silver lights, and that big giant tree with the red and yellow balls as big as basketballs. And then there were the reindeer, *real* ones. Migsy went wild over them.

I decided then that I didn't know why I never wanted to come to Washington. I mean, it's really neat being practically in the middle of history and all that. There were Migs and I wandering around all those huge Christmas trees of all the states, and maybe the President of the whole United States was looking across his garden at us from the White House. The statue of Abraham Lincoln wasn't very far off, and neither was the one of Thomas Jefferson. We were practically in the shadow of the monument to George Washington.

The only trouble was, I couldn't help wondering why all that history and greatness hadn't rubbed off on me. I went over my record since we'd arrived.

What I'm trying to say is, how far would Thomas Jefferson have got if he'd let his imagination run away with him and then been stupid enough to write it up in a theme so the whole public school system would know what a jerk he'd been? And who'd elect a President who got lost in the Pentagon? Or did a bunch of dumb stuff to make his sick mom sicker? And how about someone who got his big chance to beat up on a crummy guy and didn't do it? Would that big monument to George Washington have been there if he'd just handed a dirty handkerchief to the British to wipe their bloody noses, and then gone home? It was all pretty disgusting if you stopped to think about it.

Anyway, Migs and I stayed around the Ellipse for an hour or so. We could have stayed longer except that it was starting to rain. We wouldn't have minded snow. I had on my parka, and I'd made Migsy wear her cap and scarf and mittens. But we didn't want to hang around in the rain, so we took off for the bus. On the bus was when the one terrible thing of our whole trip happened. That was because I made the mistake of asking Migsy what she'd asked Santa Claus for. The lady sitting in front of us turned around and smiled at me.

"An alligator handbag," Migsy said.

"What do you want an alligator handbag for?" I asked without thinking.

"To get a baby brother in. I told Santa Claus I didn't want one if it didn't have a baby brother in it."

156

"What did Santa Claus say?"

"He said 'Ho! Ho! Ho!' "

I was glad he wasn't some crummy Santa Claus who promised you anything you asked for, but if I knew Migsy, she'd expect it anyway. I could see the lady in front tuning up her ears to listen in, so I dropped my voice and put my hand in front of my mouth directed toward Migsy.

"Migsy, what did I tell you about babies and alligator handbags? They don't come in alligator handbags."

Migsy stared out the window for a minute. "You never told me what kind of handbags they do come in."

"They don't come in handbags at all. Hey, look at the Bureau of Engraving and Printing. That's where they made all the money we spent today. How about that, Migs?"

"Well, what *do* babies come in? What did *I* come in?"

Migsy really had me this time, and I knew I'd have to level with her. I never wished harder in my life that it was Mom sitting next to Migsy instead of me. The lady in front of us was really having a neat time listening in. I couldn't drop my voice any lower, so I thought I'd better use sign language. I pointed to my belly button.

Then Migsy opened up in this loud voice and broadcasted to practically the whole bus, "Did I come from inside you, Andrew?" The lady in front practically had convulsions.

"No, stupid!" I hissed at her. "From inside Mom. You grew inside Mom's stomach. That's where you came from! Sheesh, Migsy!"

Suddenly Migsy looked as if she were going to bust out crying. I didn't know why until I remembered the first time I'd ever heard about it. I mean, it gives you this weird feeling to think that there you were growing right next to where your mom was probably digesting her lunch. But I didn't want Migsy crying, for Pete's sake, not after the good time we'd had and it being Christmas and all that.

"Look, Migsy," I whispered, "stop and think about it. Supposing you were born out of a handbag. Would you want to go around calling a handbag 'Mom'? Would you like to grow up to look like an alligator handbag? Maybe it would be okay if you were a baby alligator, but boyo-boy, Migsy!"

Migsy just sat with her face down, picking at her mittens.

"Look, Migs, don't you want to grow up pretty and nice and a lady like Mom? Don't you? How are you going to do that if you didn't get born out of Mom?"

Migsy sat there for forever not saying anything while I felt myself coming down with the rigor mortis. I'd said all I knew to say and I was desperate.

Finally she looked at me with this big puzzled expression. "I guess that instead I should have asked Santa Claus to have Mommy come home soon."

"You've already asked God that, haven't you?"

"Yes."

"So God will tell Santa Claus," I said.

Migsy smiled and turned to look out the window. I could tell the conversation had ended. I wiped my perspiring brow with the back of my glove.

Just then the bus stopped at the big apartments across from the Pentagon, and the lady in front of us got up to leave. She turned and gave us this big smile. She was a nosy lady, but it was a nice smile. I have to be honest.

Right after that, Migsy gave a big sigh, laid her head on my shoulder, and just looked sad and quiet. I began to worry that maybe I'd told her too much stuff all at one time.

"You okay, Migs?" I asked.

She sighed again. "I don't feel very good."

"Oh," I said cheerfully, "you'll be okay when we get home. You're just tired."

But Migsy wasn't okay when we got home. She said her throat hurt. I really knew she was sick when she started to cry after she'd asked when Mom was coming home, and I had to tell her Mom wasn't coming home right away. I didn't know anything to do then except put Migsy to bed.

It was dinnertime, so I went downstairs to fix her some soup. Mom always gives us soup when we're sick. By the time I got back upstairs with it, though, Migsy had fallen asleep. I was pretty relieved about it, because then I figured she'd just been tired after all. All I had to do was goof around until bedtime.

I plunked myself down in the living room. It looked terrible, not Christmasy or anything. We couldn't get a tree until Dad got back, because we didn't have the car to bring it in, and so far nobody had brought up the other Christmas decorations. Mom usually does that kind of stuff when she's home. There was one thing, though.

Migsy had hung up these crazy Santa Claus pictures that she'd drawn in school, but they looked sad all by themselves. I decided then that I'd do something about the living room and surprise Migsy with it in the morning, so I called Grover and we went down to the basement. I rummaged around until I finally found the boxes that had our Christmas stuff in them.

Migs and I had already moved Glorious into the basement, and he really gave Grover and me the eye while we were there. He was sitting on one of his rocks warming his back under the lamp we'd set up for him. Grover sniffed around him. Glorious kerchunked at Grover a couple of times and jumped into his pool. He was climbing back up on his rock when we left, though, and everything looked okay.

The rain was really pouring down by then. I thought again what a good thing it was Migsy and I had gotten home okay. I wondered how Beege was going to get home in it. Probably in Angela's dad's nice warm car.

I got to work right away with the tinsel and the stuffed elves and the pinecones, strewing everything around on the fireplace mantel and the tables. Then I sat down on the floor to view my work. It wasn't too hot.

I sat there listening to the rain for a while. It was really coming down, pounding on the windows like a herd of mad moose. Migsy and I had just been dying for it to snow on Christmas, all that soft, quiet, white stuff. You know, after California. Some white Christmas! Some Christmas decorations! It was pretty depressing. Grover looked at me and wagged his tail. It didn't help much. Dogs aren't very artistic. You have to face it. They like anything you do.

"Mommy!"

The rain was so noisy that I almost didn't hear the voice.

"Mommy!"

What was Migsy calling Mom for? And what was she doing waking up at ten o'clock? I took the steps up three at a time. As soon as I turned on Migsy's bed light, I could see that something wasn't right. Migsy was sitting up in bed. Her face was bright pink, and her eyes were so big that they seemed to fill up her whole face.

"I want Mommy," she said when she saw me.

"Look, Migsy, Mom's not here right now. She'll be back soon. Now, you go to sleep." I helped Migs to lie back down on her pillow. She felt like an overheated furnace.

I was scared. But I didn't want to scare Migsy. I knew I couldn't panic.

"Look, Migs," I said, "I think you're just tired from looking at all those huge Christmas trees. No kidding, we walked miles today. But just to be on the safe side, as Mom and Dad always say, why don't we play doctor and take your temperature? Okay?"

Migsy just nodded at me. She looked like one of her little Japanese dolls with the loose wooden heads. It was spooky. I ran to Mom and Dad's room to get the thermometer. All I hoped was that I could read that crazy disappearing line when I took Migsy's temperature.

I read it all right! It went to one hundred and three. I took it twice just to be sure. My stomach felt like jelly. I mean, I'm personally no M.D., but I know that nobody runs around with a reading of a hundred three, for Pete's sake. My brain went numb for a minute.

Then I thought, aspirin! You always get aspirin when you have a fever. But how much should I give Migs? And should I give her *any?* When you've been told something all your life, like never take anything out of a pill bottle unless your mom or dad tells you, you can't forget it instantly. I could just see yours truly, Andrew Kellogg, giving his sister the wrong pill. Any pill would be wrong for me. I had to face it.

I looked down at Migsy. She lay there so still and quiet. Where was my beautiful imagination? Why wasn't it telling me what to do? All it was doing was telling me what would happen to Migsy if I didn't get busy.

"I want a drink," Migsy said.

I ran to get one. It made me feel a lot better to be doing something. That's probably all Florence Nightingale did, for Pete's sake, run around getting people bunches of water.

Migsy just took a tiny sip and lay back down again. "My throat hurts. I want Mommy."

"Migsy, I can't get Mommy right now. But I'll try to get someone to help us. I'm not kidding, Migs. I'll do it. You just stay here and don't go anywhere. Okay?" I tried to smile, but it wasn't easy. Anyway, Migsy was too sick to notice.

I would have given one ear and an arm to be able to telephone Mom. But what would have been the use? I'd get her all scared for nothing. If we were still in California, there were a whole bunch of people I could have called, neighbors and stuff like that. But who was here? The person to get was Beege, if I could just find him. He was probably still with Angela, but how did I go about finding her? I knew only one place to start looking, so I headed for the High Altar in the Sacred Place. That's the dresser in Beege's room. I'm not even allowed to smell the air in his holy room without written permission. But I went there anyway. When you're desperate, you'll do anything. I found Angela's name and telephone number right away. It was on a card stuck in his mirror, written in big black letters.

I went downstairs to call. Angela's mom answered the telephone. She said Beege and Angela had been picked up by some friends and had gone to a movie. She wasn't sure which one. Did I want to leave a message? I thought about suggesting that I hoped Beege and her daughter drowned on the way to the movie, but I didn't. I just said please ask Beege to call when he got back. Then she asked me if there was anything wrong, but I said no and please just have Beege call.

Right after I hung up, though, I wished I'd said something about how Migsy and I needed help. I almost picked up the telephone and dialed the number again. But after thinking it over, I couldn't do it. She sounded pretty nice, but she was a stranger. Beege might be furious with me if I told her all our family problems, and especially how Migsy and I were all alone at home. It wouldn't make him look too neat! I couldn't call back.

I decided then that what Migsy needed was a doctor. Being a military family, we usually go to an Army or Air Force clinic. Ours here is at Fort Myer. I knew that if I called out there, they'd probably ask a bunch of questions about why I was calling and not Mom or Dad and all that. But this was an emergency, and I couldn't sit around worrying about any questions they might ask me out there. I pulled my chin down onto my neck to make my voice come out lower, picked up the telephone, and dialed Fort Myer clinic. When I told the operator what I wanted, she put me right through to the emergency room.

"U.S. Army Dispensary Emergency Room," a man's voice said. "Sergeant Tooker speaking."

"Good evening," I said. "Could I talk to a doctor, please?" With my neck down I sounded more like I was gargling than talking.

There was a dead pause at the other end of the line. "I'm sorry—uh—sir, but the doctors are all busy at the moment. Could you tell me the problem?"

"Look," I said, "my sis—I mean, I've got this sick little girl who has a temperature of about one hundred and three. I'd like to know what to do about it." I forgot to keep my chin down on my neck, and my voice ended in a high squeak.

There was another big pause. "May I ask who's calling? Are you the little girl's relative?"

"Yes," I said. Then I remembered to put my chin down and start to gargle again. "I'm—uh—Mr. Kellogg." The Kellogg came out in another squeak.

"Uh, Mr. Kellogg, may I speak with your mother or father?" the man asked. I don't blame him. I sounded like a mouse with a sore throat who just got his tail pinched in a mousetrap.

"Oh, they can't come to the phone right now," I said quickly, and I wasn't lying. "Look, couldn't I please talk to a doctor?"

"Son, it wouldn't do you any good to talk to the doctor. He'd have to see your sister. Now, I'll tell you what you do. You get your mother or father on the phone right away."

"I can't do that," I said.

"Well then, son, you tell them to please get your sister in here to the emergency room at the clinic right away. That's what the doctor would tell you if he could talk to you. Just have them bring your sister in. And be sure they bring an I.D. card."

"Okay. Thanks," I said, and hung up.

I felt sunk. How were Mom and Dad supposed to get Migsy to the clinic, for Pete's sake? With radar and an atomic-powered helicopter? Where was Beege? What was he seeing, a week-long movie? Migsy could die waiting for him. Why didn't he get home? He could take Migsy in. He had an I.D. card.

For that matter, so did I! You get one when you're ten, but you hardly ever use it then so you practically forget you have it. Why couldn't *I* take Migsy to the clinic? They'd ask a lot of questions about Mom and Dad I might not want to answer, but I'd worry about that when I got there.

When I got there! How would I get there? Who did I know who could drive us? I knew the Yellow Cab Company. I counted up my money and found I probably had enough to get us there and back. Then I called and ordered a cab, and ran upstairs to get Migsy ready.

Migsy didn't want to go. She just kept asking for Mom. I told her she had to go, because that was the only way she was going to get well. I told her about the nice doctor we'd see and the fancy cab ride we were going to have. All the time I was talking, I was pulling two sweaters on her, and a bathrobe and a jacket, three pairs of socks and a wool cap. I was working so hard I practically forgot how scared I was. What if they wouldn't take us at the clinic after all? What if I had a cab driver who wouldn't help me with Migsy? Some people won't come near you if you're sick. What if the driver thought Migsy had leprosy or something? And what if that's what she had? Oh, shut up, Cornflakes, I finally told myself. Go drown yourself!

When the cab arrived, I ran out to it, forgetting to take an umbrella and getting myself beautifully soaked. I told the cab driver my sister was sick and asked him to help me carry her out.

"Sure will, kid," he said. He never asked a single stupid question or anything. I wasn't even mad that he called me kid. He was a little guy, and he looked like an orangutan. But he was neat. People don't have to look like much to be neat. He came right up to Migsy's room, picked her up, and carried her out with me just trailing along behind holding the umbrella over them.

It wasn't until we were in the cab and I'd told him where we wanted to go that the cab driver asked me, "You alone in the house, kid?"

He'd been so nice, I found myself answering without thinking, "Yeah, I guess so."

After that I expected some more questions, but I never got any. He never even asked if I had money for the taxi. I mean, my being a kid and all that, you'd think he'd ask. All he did was start to whistle. He whistled all the way out to Fort Myer.

It wasn't a long ride, but I was half asleep by the time we got there. The cab driver stopped the cab at the clinic door, got out, and came around to get Migsy, and I didn't even know we'd stopped. He carried her in while I went up to the admissions counter.

There were a couple of guys in white jackets behind the counter. "You the patient?" one of them asked after I'd asked to see a doctor.

I guess I must have looked like it by then. "No," I said, "it's my sister."

"Are you the boy who called a little while ago?"

I nodded.

"Your mother or dad with you?"

I shook my head. I wasn't going to do any more talking than I had to.

"Well, son, you have to have something with you showing you're a military dependent."

I quickly shoved my I.D. card across the counter to him. He took it, looked at it, then looked at me again. There it was, Andrew Schofield Kellogg, born twelve years ago. He'd probably thought I was a little nine-year-old kid.

"What's your sister's name, son?"

"Mary Margaret Kellogg."

"Has she ever been in here before?"

I nodded. Mom had brought us all in for checkups before school started.

"Wait here," the man said and disappeared. In a few minutes he came back with a folder that had Migsy's name on it. "I've checked, son, and there's an authorization form here signed by your father so a doctor can treat your sister. You can wait right over there. We'll call you. It won't be long."

Authorization form, wow! I didn't even know about that, but Dad did, and whatever it was, I'd lucked out. So far so good. I hadn't had to think up a lot of answers to a lot of crummy questions. What I mean is, I didn't want to have to explain about Mom, or why I was the only one who could bring Migsy in, or any of it. All I wanted was for someone to help Migs and let us go home.

I got out my wallet to pay the cab driver.

"You want me to wait for you?" he asked.

I checked the insides of my wallet. I had just about enough to get us home without having to pay someone to wait around for us. "I guess you'd better not," I said. So I paid him for the trip out and sat down on a couch in the waiting room. He put Migsy down beside me so that her head was in my lap. Then he smiled at me and left. It's funny. I didn't even know the guy, but I really felt alone when he'd gone.

I dozed off again then, but I came to when someone lifted Migsy off my lap and I heard, "Okay, you're next, young lady!" It was another guy in a white jacket, an orderly I guess, and he carried Migsy into a doctor's office. I followed them in.

A tall, thin man with sandy-colored hair stood up. "Put her on the examining table," he told the orderly. Then he held out his hand to me, "I'm Dr. Anderson."

"Andrew Kellogg, sir," I said.

"Here, you can give me a hand," he said to me. I went over to the table, and we both started peeling off all the stuff I'd put on Migs.

"Are you this little girl's brother?" he asked.

"Yes, sir."

"Your mother or dad aren't with you?"

"Dad's on temporary duty, and Mom's sick."

Dr. Anderson motioned to me to sit down, and he started looking into Migsy's ears and down her throat and all that.

"Well, Andy, tell me this. Is there anyone else at home who can give your sister medicine?"

"Oh, I have an older brother, sir."

"Well, where is he? Is he home now?"

"Not exactly, sir."

"What do you mean, not exactly, Andy?"

"I mean, I don't exactly know where he is. Oh, it's okay, sir. Well, what I mean is, I told him I didn't mind if he went out. He doesn't know about Migsy being sick. I mean, it isn't his fault, Dr. Anderson." It wasn't a lie. I did tell Beege I didn't mind if he went out. I didn't see why I had to mention that it was two weeks ago that I'd said it. I wasn't going to make out that Beege was a crumb, for Pete's sake. He's my brother.

"I see," Dr. Anderson said in this quiet voice. I don't know what he saw, but I didn't ask. "The problem is, son, that you have a sick little girl here. I'm taking a throat culture, but in the meantime I'm going to give her an injection of penicillin. Her record shows she's not allergic to it. I'm also going to prescribe some pills, and someone has to see that she gets them. Also, I want a report first thing in the morning. When is your dad getting back from his trip?"

"Oh, he'll be home tomorrow morning, sir."

"But you don't know about your brother, do you?"

"He'll be home any minute, sir. I know he will."

"Well, I hope so. Would you like me to call and talk to your mother?"

"No, sir, it isn't necessary. I can handle it." And please let us go now, I added to myself. Don't ask any more questions.

Dr. Anderson gave me a long, close look. "All right then, Andy, but you call me immediately if your sister gets any worse, or if there's no one around your house who can help you. I may want to put her in the hospital. Now I'll have an orderly call you a cab."

It was a good thing Dr. Anderson carried Migsy out. Not that I could have done it anyway, but my knees were shaking so hard I practically had to crawl out of his office. I was never so glad in all my life as when I saw our same cab driver standing there grinning at us. I'm not kidding. He'd waited for us even when he knew I didn't have enough money for it. He took Migsy from Dr. Anderson and carried her out to the cab. When we got home, he even carried her up and helped me put her to bed. He didn't want to take his fare, either, and he was worried about leaving us alone. But I made him take the fare, and I told him we'd be okay because my brother was coming home right away.

Finally he left, and we were alone again, Migs and me.

Thirteen

Migsy dropped off to sleep right away, so I thought I'd go downstairs and take in the late movie to try to keep awake. Someone was going to have to give Migsy her medicine in a couple of hours, and if Beege didn't get back, I was going to have to be awake to do it. But what if Migsy woke up before the two hours and I didn't hear her? I decided I'd better stay right with her.

So I ended up getting a flashlight, a bottle of milk with a straw in it, a box of pretzels for Grover as well as myself, a couple of books, and a pillow. Then I made myself comfortable on the floor by Migsy's bed. It was after midnight, though, and my eyes wouldn't stay open. I must have dropped the flashlight about five times. Once it fell on my toe. That kept me awake for a while, as did

Grover snoring at my feet. But finally I dozed off anyway.

It was Grover's growling that woke me up. It was a low growl that came all the way up through him from his tail.

"Shut up," I hissed at him. "You'll wake Migsy."

Grover went right on growling. The hair down the back of his neck was standing straight up. He wasn't just kidding, and I started to get nervous, being alone and all that. I mean, the first thing you think about at a time like that, even if you have a *rotten* imagination, is that some burglar is prowling around your house. But why would anyone want to go burgling around when it was pouring down rain? I asked myself. Unless it was someone who knew that the only person in charge was a chicken twelve-year-old kid! It was a pretty disgusting thought. Also pretty terrifying. My nerves didn't feel any better when Grover suddenly jumped up and raced out of the room. I could hear him practically falling down the stairs, barking all the way. I got up and slunk out after him.

He ended up outside the door to the basement, and by the time I'd gotten to him he was busy sniffing at the bottom crack of the door. He looked up at me, barked a couple of friendly barks, wagged his tail, and started sniffing again. The burglar had to be someone Grover'd met before, someone who might know that I was alone in the house with Migsy. I slowly opened the door a crack and listened for the sounds of someone moving around, or for the breathing of someone standing there listening back at me. All I heard was a big pile of silence. Suddenly the silence was cut in two by a hollow-sounding kerchunk, kerchunk.

Grover nearly went out of his mind. He started to

whine, and before I could stop him, he pushed past my legs, spread the door open with his nose, and charged down the steps. I had a clear view of the whole basement, and with the Frog Paradise lamp still sitting on its table shining away, I could see every corner of it. There wasn't a place anyone could hide down there without at least a part of him being in view, and as far as I could see, the only burglar around was Glorious. He'd decided to take a tour of the basement and was at that moment sitting in the middle of it on a rolled-up rug, a rug that happened to be sitting in about six inches of water. It looked as if a dam had broken and the whole Potomac River had flowed in under our house.

I turned on the basement light then, and for a few minutes just stood there staring. I'd never seen a flooded basement before. It was weird. All I could think of after I'd stopped thinking about a burglar was how neat it would be to go wading in it. The water was so clear and still, like glass, and you could see all this stuff lying around under it—pictures that Mom hadn't hung up yet, an Indian rug, Dad's and Mom's golf shoes, a whole bunch of stuff. I was practically hypnotized standing there looking at it.

Finally I came to and started wondering what I could do about it. If I worked for ten years, I'd never get the water out of the basement. The only thing I could do was to rescue as much stuff as I could. What was already under water wasn't going to be improved by staying there, and with the rain still pouring down, the water level could rise and a lot more stuff could get wrecked. Like Beege's equipment box, for instance. Also a box of stuffed animals that were Migsy's and were going to be put in her room as soon as Dad got a shelf built for them. Migsy is crazy about these animals. You couldn't take a chance leaving stuff like that in the basement.

First, though, I ran upstairs to check on Migsy. She was okay, and there was still another hour before she had to have her medicine. I ran back downstairs, peeled off my socks and shoes, rolled up my pants, and waded in. I could have just put on my rubber boots, but I never think about simple things like that.

Anyway, with Grover plunging after me, I started dragging out everything that was sitting in water—the golf shoes, the pictures, a couple of sleeping bags, a bunch of filled cardboard boxes that had their bottoms soaking off. The worst job was getting the Indian rug up the stairs. It wasn't a large rug, but it was soaked through and pretty heavy. I got it pushed about halfway up the stairs and then finally quit and left it. I'd gotten everything out that had been in the water, and what was left looked safe for the moment. I decided, though, that I'd just get out Migsy's animals and Beege's stuff and then quit. I don't know why I bothered. I mean about Beege. The rotten crumb.

Getting Migsy's animals out was no sweat. But I was getting pretty tired, and Beege's equipment box was a lot bigger than I thought it was when I picked it up. I couldn't even see around it. I stumbled blind with it across the basement, and I couldn't tell when I'd reached the stairs. My foot suddenly struck the bottom step, my other foot slid out from under me, and I went down into the water. I don't know how I did it, but as I was going down I pushed the box onto a step. It hung there balancing on practically nothing.

My right ankle felt as if someone had socked it with a baseball bat, and I lay there in the water for a couple of minutes too knocked out to move. Finally I managed to get up on my knees, crawl up the steps, and steady the box. I wasn't being a big hero—I couldn't make it any farther up the steps anyway. So there I sat with Grover and Glorious, surrounded by a basement full of water, guarding a bunch of crummy sports gear. My thoughts weren't exactly beautiful, especially about Beege.

Where was he, anyway? Why wasn't he home? If he'd been there, I wouldn't have been stuck with getting all that stuff out of the basement myself. I wouldn't have had to take Migsy to the clinic myself. The rotten, lousy crumb! Where was he?

Suddenly I started to bawl.

It's a terrible thing for a twelve-year-old guy to bawl. But I couldn't stop. I think it was because I was finally admitting something to myself I'd never admitted before. When Micky stayed in California and Beege didn't have him around anymore, I thought Beege would give me the time of day for a change. Ever since I was this teeny, tiny guy, I'd always thought Beege was really the big deal, just like everyone else. But he'd always acted like I was a living, breathing example of why people have to use underarm deodorant. He practically put on nose plugs every time he saw me. I didn't understand it. Once in a while people, strangers mostly, didn't think I was so bad. Why did my own brother think I was such a jerk? Did I really stink when you got to know me?

Once you start blubbering, it's hard to stop. But I finally did. Sitting around bawling doesn't do you any good. And ankle or no ankle, I had to get back up those stairs and give Migsy her medicine. I don't know if I ever would have made it or not, because just as I was getting ready to let go of the box and hope it stayed balanced, Beege appeared at the head of the basement stairs. Naturally, the first thing he noticed wasn't the flood. It was his precious box.

"Hey, what are you doing with that?"

I didn't answer because I knew he could figure it out for himself. Besides, I didn't want to look up at him. I didn't want him to see my face and find out I'd been bawling. Then I heard him run down the stairs. "Ye gods, what's happened?"

"Look," I said, keeping my face down, "hold on to this, will you? I've got to get upstairs and give Migsy her medicine."

Beege got around me somehow and picked up the box. I tried to stand up but I couldn't. My ankle was hurting too bad.

"Hey, what's wrong? You hurt yourself?" Beege looked at my face closely then, and this strange look came into his eyes.

"I think I did something to my ankle," I said.

Beege didn't say anything. He just let go of the box and hung on to me while I got up the stairs. I heard the box slide down into the water, but he never went after it. I have to give him credit for that. When we got to the top of the stairs, he suddenly remembered something I'd said.

"What do you mean, give Migsy her medicine? Is Migsy sick?"

My ankle hurt so much by then that I could hardly think. I must have been just mumbling. "She had this high temperature. I took her—I took her to Fort Myer clinic in a—in a taxi. She has to have her—medicine. The doctor wrote down what to do. On her—bed table."

After that I guess I blacked out.

I don't remember a lot about what happened then. One-thirty in the morning has never been my best time of day even when I haven't just gone and busted my ankle. That's what I'd done, busted my crummy ankle.

Beege took over after that. He telephoned Angela's mom, and she and Angela came over and stayed with Migsy while Angela's dad drove Beege and me back to Fort Myer clinic. Angela is neat. She's pretty and nice too. I don't blame Beege. I mean, about Angela.

Anyway, at the clinic we got Dr. Anderson again. You should have seen his face when he saw me limping in and hanging on to Beege's arm. He didn't ask many questions this time, just "Is this your brother, Andy?"

"Yes, sir," I said.

"Is there someone at home taking care of your sister?"

He was talking to me, but Beege jumped in and answered, "Yes, sir. Some friends of mine are with her until we get back."

"Did she get her medicine, Andy?" Dr. Anderson asked, talking to me again. You'd think he never heard Beege.

"Yes, sir," I said.

"Andrew—uh—Andy showed me your instructions. It's being taken care of, sir," Beege said.

Dr. Anderson looked up at him and then went back to poking my ankle. "I'm glad to hear that," was all he said.

I was at the clinic for nearly two hours getting X rays

and having my ankle built into a cast. Angela and her mom stayed with Migsy, Angela's dad went on home and told us to telephone him when I was through being worked on, and Beege stayed with me. We didn't talk much, though. Beege slept most of the time, and I personally don't have anything to say anyway at that time of the day.

When we left, a guy at the front desk said, "Merry Christmas, boys!"

You know something? I'd forgotten all about it being almost Christmas.

Fourteen

IT STARTED snowing finally the next afternoon, but a heck of a lot of good it did me, with a cast all over my foot. Also, the doctor had said I ought to stick around in bed for at least a day and rest. So I was doing it.

I was also trying to read *The Hobbit*, but for some reason I wasn't too interested in it that day. Maybe it was because I was reading it for the fifth time, but I think it was mainly because I couldn't stop thinking.

My thoughts weren't very outstanding. One was about Mom. Dad had gotten back that morning and hardly said anything about her all day. He didn't act like he cared whether she ever came home or not. Maybe he was trying to soften the blow about how sick she was,

179

getting us used to not having her home for a long time—like Sally Ardery's mom. Or maybe he *really* didn't care. I couldn't help thinking about the Kogels. How did you know if your parents were about to bust up? Did they tell you and see if you liked the idea, or did they just do it? I wished I was Bilbo Baggins just running around having big adventures with Smaug the dragon and these other simple man-eating types. He didn't have stuff like parents to worry about.

Or crummy themes that make you the crummy joke of the century at school. My new school hadn't been very outstanding to start with. Now all I could think of to do was start saving coupons for a do-it-yourself hari-kari outfit. The only problem was how did a person commit it with a cast on his foot. It wouldn't be easy.

And last but not least, there was Beege. Ever since Dad got back, Beege was racing around giving Migsy her medicine and everything, just like he'd been managing the show the whole time. I didn't think he'd ever tell Dad any of it, what really happened, and he knew I wouldn't either. He was pretty safe keeping his mouth shut.

Anyway, I'd hardly seen him since the night before. Micky had gotten in from California that morning about the same time as Dad, and he and Beege had been gone all afternoon. I hadn't seen Beege since he'd brought me up a crummy peanut-butter sandwich at noon. Big deal.

I guess I wouldn't have cared so much if only he'd said thanks for anything. I knew he'd sat up all night with me at the clinic, but that wasn't it. It was all the rest of it. I swear I wouldn't have cared about anything if he'd just said thanks once.

At any rate, I finally gave up on the book and turned on the transistor radio by my bed. Grover and I were listening to Christmas music when Dad came into my room. He'd been down working on the basement—*without* the help of Beege and Micky, I'd noticed.

"How's it going, son?" Dad asked, sitting on the edge of my bed and giving the cast on my leg a friendly pat.

"Oh, okay, I guess," I said. That's what you always say when people ask you about the condition you're in even if you don't mean it.

Dad could tell I wasn't meaning it. "Well," he said, giving my cemented-in leg another pat, "I don't blame you for feeling a little down. It's a bum rap, sitting up here with a cast on your leg when all that snow is coming down."

I didn't tell Dad it wasn't just the snow that was bugging me. "Yeah," I said.

"Anyway," he went on, "I picked up a nice tree this morning and a good fat turkey, an eighteen pounder. Beege is going to help me stuff it and roast it tomorrow. I guess you boys picked up a lot of cooking experience while I was gone, didn't you?"

"Oh sure," I said, remembering how much experience Beege had picked up, not in cooking, however.

"Which reminds me," Dad said, "you know I haven't had a chance to talk to you, Andrew, since I got back this morning."

"You're not mad at us, are you, Dad?" I asked. "I mean, not letting you know about Josie getting sick and all that?"

"No, I'm not mad at you. You did what you thought

was right, and I'm not sure I wouldn't have done the same thing in your shoes. I'm grateful that you're intelligent boys and could handle the emergencies. I had a long talk with your brother, and he explained everything that happened right from the beginning. And I repeat, Andrew, I'm not mad at either of you."

Not mad at *either* of us. I couldn't help checking that. "What—what exactly did Beege tell you, Dad?"

"Nothing special, son. As I said, just a rundown of what happened." Dad shrugged and looked blank. "Why?"

"Oh, no reason," I said. "Just asking."

I could tell from Dad's ignorant expression just what kind of rundown Beege had given him. Well, heck, it wasn't that I expected a big hero medal or anything like that. Anyway, what had I done so great except bake Migsy a rotten strawberry cake and deliver a couple of lectures on sex education? But I have to be honest. I would have liked a little pat on the head. I mean, I give Grover a pat on the head when he just looks up at me and drools, for Pete's sake.

Dad rose from my bed. "Well, back to the drawing board!"

"Dad?"

"Yes, son?"

"It's about Mom. When do you think she's coming back?"

Dad got the same blank look on his face. "Well, Andrew, I don't really—" he began. And then you wouldn't believe it, but the doorbell rang. It wasn't the school bell, but it was a miracle just the same, for Dad anyway. You could tell he hadn't wanted to talk about Mom. He grinned when the doorbell rang. I almost hated him when he went down to answer it.

I picked up my book, but I wasn't reading it, only staring at it.

"How!"

I hadn't heard anyone come in with the radio going, but here was this guy standing there with his arm raised in an Indian salute. This was pretty strange when you considered that the guy was Chinese.

I couldn't think of anything to do, so I raised my arm right back at him and said, "How!"

"Congratulations," said the guy. "I see you're an American Indian, too." Then he smiled and held out his hand. "Shake. My name's Bobby Lee."

"Hi," I said. "Have a seat."

Bobby pulled off his coat and plunked down on my window seat. "Hey," he said, "I'm really glad I found out who you were. You know, through that crazy theme. What a sense of humor, man!"

"Uh, thanks," I said.

"Don't mention it. My grandmother was losing her mind wanting to know who that lunatic was that she met in the garden. 'The South will rise again, ma'am!' You really killed her."

"I nearly killed myself," I said.

"So I notice. Hey, you didn't do that in *our* place, did you?"

"Heck no! In my own basement."

"Whew, that's a relief! Grandmother would die if you had. You know, honorable Oriental hospitality and all that jazz."

"Uh, listen," I said, "did your grandmother actually *read* that stuff I wrote?"

"No. She just heard about it from me. But don't worry about it. She thinks it's great. She's crazy to meet you. I think she's planning to have you over to dinner and serve you egg rolls over hominy grits, sweet and sour hush puppies, and Southern-fried fortune cookies."

"She's kidding!" I said.

"Listen, my grandmother never kids about anything."

"Well, tell your grandmother I accept," I said.

"Good, but what I really came over for is to invite you to this party I'm having New Year's Eve. It's going to be in that basement gymnasium where you saw my cousin giving me a fencing lesson. Outside of that, I hardly use it. My pop is a physical fitness nut, and he says I'm going to start using it or else. So I'm starting by having a party in it. Can you come?"

"I'd like to," I said, "but how can I with this on my leg?"

"No problem. We'll arrange it. Glad you can come! Maybe later when you're rid of that oversized Band-Aid, you can come over and we'll really give the gym a workout. Hey, by the way, what's with you and Sally Ardery?"

"Nothing's with me and Sally Ardery," I said. I mean, I had to be honest, there really wasn't anything that I knew of.

"Well, she asked me if you were coming to the party,

and I told her I was planning to ask you. Just thought you'd like to know."

"Yeah," I said.

Bobby jumped up from the window seat and threw his coat back on. "Look, I've got to go now. I promised Pop I'd come right back. So, be seeing ya." He gave his Indian salute and left. In a couple of seconds, he poked his head back through the doorway. "By the way, rumor has it that you're going to be asked to write the seventh-grade class play this year—or do something with it anyway."

"I haven't heard that rumor," I said.

"You will," said Bobby. "See ya!"

There was no denying that life looked a whole lot better after that. Not perfect, considering the way things were in my family, but a lot better. At least my estimation of my crummy self had risen a little. If only it would rise in the eyes of that one rotten brother of mine. But I was resigned to that never happening. You get stuck in a family and you get what you get. I was going to have to face it.

And then there was still the matter of Mom. I couldn't help it—I started worrying again.

Anyway, the next day was Christmas.

Migsy was just well enough Christmas morning to come downstairs for breakfast and the tree. She wasn't well enough to go out, though, so because of my ankle and her being sick, we didn't get to church. Dad said no presents, though, until he'd read us some stuff from the Bible and we'd had breakfast. He fixed us some waffles, which weren't too bad considering Dad had made them.

Besides, you can eat anything when you're really hungry.

While we were eating, Dad acted very fidgety and nervous, like he was expecting the house to blow up. About nine o'clock the doorbell rang.

"Go get the telephone, will you, Beege?" Dad said.

"Dad, get with it," Beege said. "That's the doorbell."

"Oh, is it?" Dad said. He sounded like he'd lost his marbles. We kids all looked at each other and shrugged. "Well then," Dad said to Beege, "go get the door."

Beege did, and came back into the dining room with Mom.

Everybody just sat and stared. Nobody seemed to believe it. Except Dad and Micky, and their faces were covered with these huge grins. They were the only ones who knew it was going to happen.

"Well, isn't anybody going to do anything?" Mom said. Migsy jumped up, ran over, and threw her arms around Mom's neck. That started it. Micky went over, and Mom hugged *him* so hard I thought she'd break him. Then Dad went and hugged *Mom*. Her eyes were wet with tears. Like I said before, I hate to see Mom cry, but it's different when she's laughing at the same time. And Mom was laughing. It was okay.

I wanted to go and hug Mom too, but I couldn't. It wasn't because of my ankle either. I get pretty shy about stuff sometimes. But Mom saw me standing around and raced over to *me*. She squeezed me so hard I thought I'd end up with my neck in a cast, too.

"Oh, Andrew! Andrew!" was all she said, but she didn't have to say anything else. You know, sometimes you get this screwy idea that people in your family, like your mom and dad, don't like you as well as someone else in the family. Especially if you're not the big deal and your rotten subconscious keeps reminding you of it. But I knew then that Mom wasn't any happier about seeing Micky or Beege or Migsy, than she was me. You can suddenly tell stuff like that.

After all the hugging and kissing and all that boloney, we went into the living room. Then Aunt Ann, who'd driven Mom down from New York, came in, and everyone started talking at once. That was when we found out how Dad knew that Mom was coming. He'd stopped in New York on his way home and they'd decided it then. Dad had telephoned Mom Christmas Eve, too, to make sure everything was okay and to tell her about Migsy being sick and me having a cast on my foot.

Suddenly, after we'd finished all those subjects, no one could think of anything to say. We all just sat looking at each other.

Then Migsy shouted out, "Mommy, Mommy, we had a swimming pool in our basement!"

"A swimming pool?"

"What it was, Mom," Beege said, "was a flooded basement."

"But it's okay, Sam," Dad added quickly. "The water's gone down. You remember I told you that Andrew had broken his ankle on the basement stairs. What I didn't mention was that it happened when he was performing a rescue operation on some of our prized possessions—our golf shoes for a couple of things. But don't worry about it. Outside of Andrew's ankle, it's all cleaned up now."

I guess we were all kind of looking at Mom to see how she was taking this piece of news. A couple of months ago hearing about a flooded basement would have made her hysterical. The living room grew pretty quiet. Then Mom started to laugh.

"So, you kids got your swimming pool after all. And indoors yet! Great heavens, you don't think the basement will have the nerve to flood again, do you?"

"That's just it, Sam," Dad said. "It's flooded before, and I haven't much doubt that it will again. I think we're going to have to have some work done before long and it's not going to be cheap. There goes your new kitchen for a while."

Mom laughed again, pulling Migsy onto her lap. "Don't you dare mention a new kitchen! I love that old place just the way it is. I don't know how I'd survive the boredom of getting dinner without wondering what weapon was going to hurl out and smash me to bits. You have no idea how I missed all the excitement while I was helping Ann cook in her nice, ordinary, safe kitchen!"

After that we all *knew*. Maybe not right then, but one day soon, Mom would be home to stay. No one had to tell us. As for Dad, well, you could see how he felt. I don't know where I ever got the idea about him not caring. You can really imagine a lot of wild stuff if you just set your mind to it.

Anyway, after that we started opening our presents, and while we were doing it, Beege and Micky got up and left the room. Before long they came back carrying this big package. I mean, it was *really* big. They sat it down in front of me. I just sat staring at it.

"Well, open it, stupid," said Micky.

"You mean it's for me?"

"Why don't you open it and find out," Micky said.

Beege had picked up the book I'd given him and was calmly reading. Too calmly. I figured something *very* funny was going on.

I ripped the paper off, and there was this brand-new three-speed bicycle. Hanging from the handlebars was a card.

"Read it out loud! Read it out loud!" Migsy shouted, jumping around like a grasshopper.

"To Andy," I read, "the not-so-absentminded professor, with thanks for services rendered. Beege."

I looked at Beege. He was still pretending to read his book. I looked at Dad. He gave me the same blank look he'd given me up in my room, only this time he added a big, solemn wink. Beege must have told him all of it. He'd known all along, just as he'd known all along that Mom was on her way home for Christmas. What a crumb that Dad of mine was! I mean, a *nice* crumb!

"I want you to appreciate the fact, my friend," Micky said, "that I gave up most of yesterday running around town with that madman brother of yours finding that bicycle. I'll tell you it ain't easy finding a decent vehicle the day before Christmas, but he wouldn't give up. We must have covered ten stores!"

"Wow!" I said, testing the bike's hand brakes. I wanted to say a lot more, but I couldn't. Everyone was looking at me except Beege, who was kindly pretending to be reading the book, and my crummy ears were getting hot.

"Speech! Come on, let's have a speech, professor," Micky yelled.

Beege finally looked up from the book. "Oh, shut up, Micky. Leave him alone!"

Micky shrugged. "Sure. Sure."

"Well, let's get back to the rest of the tree," Dad said quickly. "Come on, Migs, you finish playing Santa Claus."

Migsy giggled and ran to the tree. Then she stooped down and picked up a white envelope. "It's a letter for A-n-d-r-e-w K-e-l-l-o-g-g." She spelled my name out. "What's a letter for Andrew doing under the tree?"

"My fault," Dad said. "I don't know how it got under there, but I was on my way up with it last night and I guess I got sidetracked. Sorry, son."

Migsy handed me this big, fat envelope, and in it were a card, a letter, and a picture. The picture was of a guy hanging from a tree with his eyes crossed, and he was scratching under his arms monkey style. The letter said the guy wished I'd get back to California because he was tired of hanging there all by himself. He said everyone thought he was nuts. He is, too. I'm not kidding. The guy who wrote the letter was Jay.

"Well," I said, "whadya know!" It was all I could think of at the moment.

Barbara Brooks Wallace was born in Soochow, China, and had crossed the Pacific nine times before coming to live in the United States. Her father was an American businessman and her mother had been a nurse in Shanghai, where they met and married.

Mrs. Wallace writes that she and her sister were "always closely guarded by amahs and Mother, but the first time Mother ever let us out of her sight—which was to allow us to leave Shanghai under the care of a lady missionary doctor to spend the summer in Peitaho—the 'unofficial' Japanese war flared up and we were totally cut off from Shanghai. Mother and Dad were evacuated to the Philippines from Shanghai, and later, my sister and I were evacuated from Peitaho on an American destroyer."

Mrs. Wallace attended schools in China and graduated from U.C.L.A. She met her husband, an air force officer and West Point graduate, in Santa Monica. They now live in Virginia with their son Jimmy.